MW01241683

TREASURE ISLAND

By Robert Louis Stevenson

Adapted for the stage By

Vernon Morris

In collaboration with

B H BARRY

ISBN: 978-1-6847-1255-7 (sc)
ISBN: 978-1-6847-1254-0 (e)

Lulu Publishing Services rev. date: 11/11/2019

It was Christmas Day, many years ago, and we were snowed in on a mountain top in Wales. We had all lunched well and the adults were taking a nap. My aunt kindly read to me a story from a book I'd been given earlier that morning. Suddenly, I was magically taken away from the freezing cold and misty mountain into a world of sunshine, warm water, tropical islands and pirates hunting for gold. That wonderful Christmas has stayed with me my whole life.

When B H Barry said to me he was looking for a play to produce, I suggested Treasure Island, a script that I had been working on for some time. Together we had a great fun working on this wonderful story and bringing it to life for the stage. Hope when are you reading this script you will have as much pleasure from it as we did in creating it.

Playwright
Vernon Morris

About the play

It seems as if Treasure Island, by Robert Louis Stevenson, has always been a part of my life. I read it as a child, I saw many movie versions with such actors as Robert Newton, Orson Welles, Wallace Beary, Jack Palance, even Eddie Izzard, all playing Long John Silver, all magnificent in their own way.

In the early sixties Bernard Miles played Long John Silver at The Mermaid Theatre in London. I later choreographed that production at The Mermaid, and also at the Chichester Festival Theatre.

With our version of the story, and after directing it at The Ohio Theater in New York City, The Pirate Playhouse on Sanibel Island and finally at the Irondale Theater Center in Brooklyn, I believe Vernon and I have come up with the best possible version.

The play, in two acts, moves with a smoothness that makes an evening in the theater a celebration of storytelling and drama. The sea chanteys are easily accessible on the web, I have not included all the lyrics or the music; they are all in the public domain.

Vernon Morris, my collaborator and partner in crime, and I have tried to remain as close to the the book as possible. We both love the language that Stevenson used and although we have been pressured to "Americanize" the script, we have resisted. The language is so much a part of the original book that it is a major factor in its magic.However, I have included an idex, realizing some of the terminology is confusing.

The story explores a young person's right of passage. This universal human condition speaks to all genders and races about choosing right from wrong. Making the right choice no matter how seductive the wrong choice is.Jim Hawkin's dilemma has faced all of us at sometime in our youth. What makes this a classic tale is that it transcends time. It is universal.

"And you m'lay to that!"

Producer / Director

B H Barry

CAST LIST

Long John Silver	Tom Hewitt
Jim Hawkins	Noah Galvin
Dr Livesey	Rocco Sisto
Squire Trelawney	Kenneth Tigar
Smollet	Steve Blanchard
Billy Bones / Morgan	John Ahlin
Black Dog / George Merry	Michael Gabriel Goodfriend
Mr. Arrow / Tom/ Pirate	Josh Clayton
Blind Pew/ Ben Gunn	Tom Beckett
Israel Hands/ Flint	Rod Brogan
O'Brien / Allerdyes	Liberty Smiling
Chantey man/ Pirate / Mrs. Hawkins / Redruth	Ken Schatz
Dirk	Philip Willingham

Long John Silver-Tom Hewitt

Jim Hawkins-Noah Galvin

Front Row: Noah Galvin (Jim) Tom Hewitt (Silver)

Back row: Philip Willingham (Dirk) Ken Schatz (Chanty man)
Liberty Smiling (O'Brien)

Director- B H Barry

Lighting Designer- Stewart Wagner
Scenic Designer- Tony Straiges
Costume Designer- Luke Aaron
Sound Designer-Will Pickens
Special Effects- Greg Meeh
Music Director -Ken Schatz
Photos -Ken Howard
Logo -Achilles Lavidis
Assistant Fight Director-Brad Lemons
Assistant to the Director-Penny Bergman
Fight Director-B H Barry

Character Descriptions

Parts with no doubles.

Jim Hawkins — Everybody's idea of a young 13-year-old boy. Cornish looking. Round open-faced innocent, playing down to 13 or 15. Depending on the age of Long John. Jim could be a fifteen year old if Long John were in his fifties. The older Long John, the younger Jim.

Squire Trelawney — Squire is the heart.
Overly enthusiastic on everything he does. Not a mean bone in his body. Spoilt but not petulant. His belief is that money solves everything.

Smollet — Smollet is the hands.
He provides the action. Very much a 50's type. King and country and all that. Rough and ready for action. Errol Flynn.

Dr Livesey — Dr. Livesey is the head,
Country Doctor. Logical and sensible.

Silver — Incorporates all the qualities of the three good guys. Totally amoral Santa Clause with a knife. Everybody's uncle. Sociopath.

Dirk — Youngest of the pirates, over compensates.
Wants to be accepted. 20's. Small

Doubles

Billy Bones	Big and powerful, he is used to being obeyed. Has to fight. Good example, Oliver Reede. 50s.
Morgan	Helpful type. Lawyer. Welsh. Older.
Black Dog	Not too threatening but can take care of himself.. Oily. 30's.
George Merry	Next in line to be captain after Long John.Lawyer, Is always right.
Tom.	He is the Squire's gardener. Simple and to the point.
Pirate	Has to be a fighter.
Arrow	Ex naval man. Sadistic. Silver's front man to Captain Smollet. Bully. Rough.
Blind Pew	Creepy, blind, Welsh accent 50's. A good double with Ben Gunn
Ben Gunn	Weird! Weird! Been too long on his own. He has spent the last three years on the island living with goats. He found a parasol.Robin Williams type
Israel Hands	Ruthless, gift of the gab.30's. Must be buff. Could be Irish.

Cap'n Flint	Ruthless, It would be hard to argue with him on any topic.
O'Brien	Was a farmer, got the bad end of a deal. Not too smart, lots of attitude. 30's. Must be buff. Irish accent.
Allerdyes	Great friend of Captain Flint. Scottish.
Redruth	Loyal servant to the Squire.
Mrs Hawkins	Tough, not to be messed around with. Country type.
Parrot	Should have feathers and be able to sit on a shoulder.
Chantey man	Singer of sea chanteys.

Flint and Four pirates at beginning.
All these characters should represent
the richest of pirates.They have
dressed themselves as
fighting cocks.

ALL SCENES AND TRANSITIONS ARE CREATED BY THE USE AND REARRANGEMENT OF SIMPLE SCENIC ELEMENTS: ROLLING PLATFORMS, BARRELS, ROPES AND SMALL PROPS-ALL OF WHICH ARE MOVED BY THE ACTORS. AT THE TOP OF THE PLAY THE AUDITORIUM HAS THE LOOK OF AND FEEL OF A CORNISH INN,

ACT ONE

PROLOGUE

The stage surface is covered with a silk onto which we shine a gobo of water. Waves gently move across the space. While the audience is entering the auditorium, the lights and sound cycle through the play-from Cornwall to Skeleton Island. On the cyclorama behind the audience is projected a representation of the moors. All images will be representational in the style of the artist Turner. The house lights dim, a rumble of thunder is heard.
A wind picks up and the sails and ropes above the audience's heads begins to stir. The effects will increase in momentum culminating in a crash of thunder. The gobo on the silk slowly begins to spin into a whirlpool. It fills with air and we see TREASURE ISLAND by Robert Louis Stevenson written on it. The silk gets bigger and bigger, forming the roof of the cave. Captain Flint and the pirates are discovered on stage in a cloud of smoke.

A CAVE

FLINT
Come on mates, get a move on. Put those barrels
of coins with the rest of the treasure.
ALLERDYCE
Let's have another look, Captain Flint.
*Flint opens treasure chest. Special effects
glow emits from the chest.*
Lovely! Diamonds, pearls, look at this
emerald. A King's ransom!
FLINT
Pretty to see, ain't it?
ALLERDYCE
It's our security, right? For all of us to live like kings.

1

FLINT

Oh, yes! When the time comes we will be living
like royalty, lads. Those of that is left.

PIRATE 1

Right you, are Cap'n Flint.

PIRATE 3

I think it's stupid to leave the treasure
here. Someone might find it.

PIRATE 2

Rushes in

Cap'n Flint, Cap'n Flint.

FLINT

Speak up lad what is it?

PIRATE 2

Those two English frigates that's been following us have just
been sighted on the other side of the island on the north inlet.

FLINT

Now you know why I wanted to leave the treasure
in this 'ere cave. Our only chance to escape is
to lighten the ship so we can sail it over the reef
before high tide. We'd better budge, mates.

PIRATE

I still think we should take some of it with
us. Putting it in a cave is stupid.

Flint shoots him.

FLINT

Anyone else got any opinions.

OTHER PIRATES

No, no, no Cap'n.

A flash of lighting. A crash of thunder.

Lock it up, boyo. Now back to the ship with ye. Allerdyce
and I will finish up here. Don't want to miss the tide,
do we? Take the path along the cliff. It's quicker.

PIRATES

Right you are, Cap'n Flint....Etc

They exit.

The ropes have been tied together with twine
to look like the ropes of a bridge.

ALLERDYCE

(With mock surprise.)

The cliff path? That means they have to cross over that old
rotting rope bridge. Do you think it will hold their weight?

Flint draws his cutlass, Allerdyce does the same.

FLINT

Course it will.

They both raise their cutlasses and cut through the twine
holding the ropes together.The ropes snake off stage.
We hear the pirates scream as they fall to their death..

FLINT

(ironically)

But then, of course I could be wrong! That just leaves
you and me who knows where this 'ere treasure is.

ALLERDYCE

He closes the lid and snaps the lock shut.

We'd better mark this cave so as we
can find the treasure again.

FLINT

What we need is a pointer. That's what we need, a pointer.

ALLERDYCE

We should have brought something from the ship.

FLINT

Ah, there's a slipped hitch.

Taking out a flask of brandy.

You and me is like two peas in a pod. Here, have a drink out
of little Davy Jones.I need to think about this 'ere pointer.

Allerdyce drinks. Flint draws a knife and cuts Allerdyce's
throat, spins him around and plunges the knife into his
stomach. He then lays him out as a pointer on the platform.

3

FLINT

Thank you Allerdyce, you got the point nicely, my son.

Flint takes a barrel of gunpowder over to the entrance of the cave. He lights the fuse.

Dead men tell no tales.

Fuse is burning as......

SHANTY MAN

FIFTEEN MEN ON A DEAD MAN'S CHEST
YO! HO! HO! AND A BOTTLE OF RUM
DRINK AND THE DEVIL HAVE DONE FOR THE REST
YO! HO! HO! AND A BOTTLE OF RUM.

Explosion. Smoke. Echoing sound. Projected onto the cyclorama explosion images. The silk vanishes. Change Cyclorama to moors. Smoke fills the stage.

ADMIRAL BENBOW INN

JIM

My name is Jim Hawkins and I am going to relate to you the events that changed my life. The first time I heard that song was when an old seaman called Captain Billy Bones came plodding to our inn door, his sea chest following behind him in a hand barrow. Hearing our inn well spoken of and described as lonely, he chose it as his place of residence.

Jim and the Shanty man start setting up the inn using the on stage barrels tables etc. Jim continues speaking.

We were glad to have him as a paying guest as we were in need of the money — my father being very ill and bedridden at the time. All day long the captain stood on the cliffs with a brass telescope, searching the horizon.

Lights come up on Billy Bones

Every day he would ask...

BILLY BONES

Have you seen any sea-faring men going along the road? I promise you a silver forpenny on the first of every month if you would keep *your* "weather-eye" open for a seafaring man with one leg. Remember him above all.

JIM

Many's the night that I had terrifying dreams about a one-legged, seafaring man. It was one January morning; the captain had risen early and I was laying the breakfast table against his return, when a stranger entered our inn.

Black Dog enters with great stealth and
makes his way to the table.

JIM

Looks up with a start.

Oh, I'm sorry, sir, I didn't hear you come in. What would be your pleasure?

BLACK DOG

I'll take a glass of rum.

JIM

At once, sir.

Jim gets the drink. Black Dog motions
Jim to bring the drink to him.

BLACK DOG

Come here, sonny. Come nearer here.

Jim takes a step nearer.

Is this here table for my mate Bill?

JIM

I'm sorry, sir, I don't know your mate, Bill. The table is set for our paying guest, whom we call the captain.

BLACK DOG

Well, yes, my mate, Bill would be called the captain, as like as not. He has a cut on one cheek — and we'll put it, if you like, that that cheek's the right one. Now, is my mate Bill in this house?

JIM

If indeed it be he, sir, he's out walking.

BLACK DOG
Which way, sonny? Which way is he gone?
JIM
Up to the big rock on the cliff; he goes there every
day. But he'll be back soon for his breakfast. I'll
run and tell him he has a friend waiting.
BLACK DOG
There'll be no need of that. I'll just wait here till he returns.
JIM
It'll be no trouble, sir. I'll be there and back in a flash.
Jim makes for the door, but Black Dog beats him to it.
BLACK DOG
Shouting
I said, there'll be no need!
Jim backs into the room.
I've taken quite a shine to ye.
Patting Jim's shoulder.
But the great thing for boys is discipline.
Looking off.
Well, sure enough, here is my mate, Bill, with a spy-
glass under his arm, bless his old 'art, to be sure.
*Black Dog drags Jim to a corner of the bar. Billy Bones enters
singing "Fifteen Men on a Dead Man's Chest" and goes
straight past them to the table and sits with his back to them.*
BLACK DOG
Bill!
Billy almost falls as he jumps up.
BILLY
Who the...?
BLACK DOG
Come on, Bill, you know me; you know
an old ship-mate, Bill, surely?
BILLY
(Horrified)
Black Dog, by thunder!

BLACK DOG
And who else? You know what I come for, Bill.
BILLY
(Frightened)
Aye.
BLACK DOG
Flint's Fist!
BILLY
(Bluffing)
Then you tell them lubbers as sent you, that
I'm still captain, and, being in charge, I...
BLACK DOG
Not any more, Billy Bones, me boy'o. We'll
be giving you the black spot!
BILLY
So be it! Give me the black spot if you dare. If you think
you're man enough! Flint's map stays with me. Now,
tell that to the crew. Flint's map stays in my hands!
BLACK DOG
You'll be sorry, Bill Bones. The crew's not to be crossed.
BILLY
No more am I. Now get out before I run you through!
BLACK DOG
The map rightfully belongs to us, Flint's
crew. And you've no right to...
BILLY
Drawing his cutlass.
Get out of here, you yellow-bellied son of a...
BLACK DOG
Making for the door.
We'll see you swing for this, Billy Bones!
BILLY
I'll see you dead first...!
Billy attacks Black Dog. They fight.

BLACK DOG

Now, Billy, be reasonable...

*Jim watches in horror as they slash at each
other until Black Dog retreats. Jim runs out
after Black Dog. Mrs.Hawkins enters.*

MRS.HAWKINS

For heaven's sake, what's going on here? Captain...
please put that sword away and quiet down.

BILLY

More rum, good and strong!

MRS. HAWKINS

Please, Captain! If you keep drinking
rum the way you do, you'll die!

BILLY

You can take a long run off a short plank, for all I care!

MRS. HAWKINS

Shhhh! Will you!

BILLY

More rum!

MRS. HAWKINS

Be it on your own head.

BILLY

Get me rum at once, I say!

MRS. HAWKINS

Please, Captain, no more. My husband is
desperately ill and needs quiet.

BILLY

Shouting

You be quiet, woman!

*JIM and DR. LIVESEY enter from the
father's room. He crosses to Billy.*

DR. LIVESEY

No, Captain Bones, you be quiet.

BILLY

Hold your tongue or I'll have you flogged!

DR. LIVESEY

Are you addressing me, sir? I have only one thing
to say to you — if you keep drinking rum, the world
will soon be quit of a very dirty scoundrel!

*Billy, livid with rage, pulls out his sword. Knocking over
the barrel in front of him, he advances on Dr. Livesey.*

If you do not put that sword back, I promise, upon
my honor, you shall hang at the next assizes.

*Billy looks dangerous for a moment or two, then,
grumbling to himself, he lowers his sword. Dr.
Livesey crosses to Mrs.Hawkins and Jim.*

I'm not only a doctor but also a magistrate...

Billy throws his cutlass down.

....and if I catch a breath of a complaint against
you, I'll take effectual means to have you hunted
down and routed out. Do I make myself clear?

*Billy stares at the doctor for a moment,
then he exits out the door.*

MRS.HAWKINS

Thank you, Dr. Livesey.

DR. LIVESEY

Any more trouble from the likes of him and
I'll lay him by the heels. My coat, Jim.

Jim gets Dr.Livesey's coat.

MRS. HAWKINS

Good-day, sir.

Helping Livesey on with his coat.

And thank you for all your help.

DR. LIVESEY

Anytime, Mrs. Hawkins. Good day, Jim.

The lights dim down as Dr.Livesey and Mrs. Hawkins exit.

JIM

That night, my father died.

*Two men enter with the body of Jim's
father and cross the stage.*

CHANTEYMAN

**IN THE BLUSTEROUS WIND IN THE DARK WATERS
A SHIP WENT DRIFTING ON THE SEA....**

JIM

The undertaker arrived in the morning to collect the body.
It was a miserable day, raining, bible black and stormy.

CHANTEYMAN

Sings rest of chantey.

***HER HEADGEAR GONE HER RUDDER
BROUGHT HER TO
EXTREMITY.***

JIM

Makes noise with the tankards.

The captain slept till the early afternoon.

BILLY

Waking up.

Jim!

JIM

Yes, sir.

BILLY

What time is it?

JIM

Three o'clock.

Jim kneels down by Billy.

BILLY

I've got to get away from here. They're after Flint's map,
Jim. Bring me a noggin of rum, there's a good lad.

JIM

But, Captain, the doctor said...

BILLY

Jim sits down by the fireplace. Billy sits on table.

Doctors is all swabs. What do they know about sea-
faring men? I've lived on rum, I tell you. It's been man

and wife to me. Look how my fingers fidges. I can't keep
'em still. I'll give you a golden guinea for a noggin, Jim.

JIM

Getting rum.

I want none of your money but what you owe my
mother. I'll get you one glass and no more.

Jim brings a glass to Billy.

BILLY

Thank you, mate. They are going to give me the black spot.

JIM

What's the black spot?

BILLY

He looks around the bar to make sure no one is listening.

It's my old sea-chest they're after and Flint's map
within it. We'll beat them yet. I was old Flint's first
mate, and I'm the only one as knows the place.

JIM

What place, Captain?

BILLY

The place where Flint hid his treasure—he gave
me his map. We call it Flint's Fist! He gave it me at
Savannah, when he lay a-dying. But don't tell anyone
unless they get the black spot on me.

JIM

But what is the black spot, Captain?

BILLY

Bless you, Jim. It's a bit o' paper with orders
from the crew when they want to
replace their captain. But you keep a weather-eye
open, Jim, for that Black Dog or a sea-faring man
with one leg. Remember him above all. If you do all
this, I'll share with you equals, upon my honor.

CHANTEYMAN
Sings
**LOOK AHEAD, LOOK ASTERN, LOOK
A WEATHER AND A LEE.
BLOW HIGH, BLOW LOW, AND SO SAILED WE.
FOR WE ARE A SALT SEA PIRATE ALL
A LOOKING FOR OUR FEE.
SAILING DOWN ALONG THE COAST
OF THE HIGH COUNTRY.**

Billy settles back in his chair and falls asleep. We hear the tapping of a stick. A knock comes from the front door. A storm is brewing. Jim lights a lamp. He crosses out of the bar, taking the lamp with him and goes to the front door. As Jim opens the door, Blind Pew is standing in the lamplight. Jim gasps at the sight. Blind Pew is a dreadful looking figure, holding a white stick and wearing a green shade over his eyes and nose. He is clad in a huge, tattered, old sea cloak with a hood. He speaks in an odd singsong sort of way. (Welsh accent.)

PEW
Will any kind friend inform a poor blind man, who lost the precious sight of his eyes in the gracious defense of his native country, England — and God bless King George! —where or in what part of the country he may now be?

JIM
You are at the Admiral Benbow, Black
Hill Cove, my good man.

PEW
I hear a voice, a sweet, young voice. Will you give me your hand, my kind young friend, and lead me in?
Jim holds out his hand. Pew grabs it in a vise-like grip.

PEW
Now, boy, take me to the captain.

JIM
Sir, upon my word I dare not!

PEW
Take me in straight or I'll break your arm.
JIM
Ahhh!
PEW
Come, now, march. Lead me straight to him,
and when I'm in view cry out, "Here's a friend
for you, Bill." If you don't do it, I'll do this!
He wrenches Jim's arm.
JIM
Ahhhhh!
Jim and Pew cross to Billy. Jim holds up the lamp.
Pew, in this light, should look quite cadaverous.
Captain, there's someone to see you.
Billy opens his eyes, sees Pew, and recoils in horror.
BILLY
Pew!
PEW
Now, Bill, sit where you are. If I can't see, I can hear a finger
stirring. Business is business. Hold out your left hand. Boy,
take his left hand by the wrist and bring it near to my right.
He gives Billy the black spot.
There, that's done. We want that map, Flint's Fist,
and we'll have it, Billy. I'll be back with the boys.
With sudden swiftness Pew is out of the bar area
and across the hall and through the front door. We
can hear him with his stick tap tapping away.
BILLY
Standing
We'll do them yet!
Billy suddenly puts a hand to his throat, sways for a
moment, then gasps and falls dead on the floor.

JIM

Running to Billy.

Captain...

Mrs. Hawkins enters and sees Jim trying to wake Billy.

Captain...! Mother!

MRS HAWKINS

Oh, no, not again. I won't stand for it! Sick or not....!

JIM

Jim is listening for a heartbeat.

(With great sadness)

I think he's dead!

MRS. HAWKINS

(Realizing what this means financially)

Dead! Oh no, and him owing us all that
money! What are you doing, boy?

JIM

Looking for a key, Mother.

MRS. HAWKINS

A key?

JIM

Yes, to the captain's sea chest.

*Jim opens Billy's shirt and finds the key around his neck. Jim
cuts the cord, takes the key and, grabbing a nearby lantern,
crosses the stage to the area designated as Billy's room.*

MRS. HAWKINS

Now what are you doing?

JIM

I'm looking for Flint's Fist.

*He opens the sea chest and finds a bag of
money which he gives to his mother.*

MRS. HAWKINS

I'm an honest woman. I'll have my dues and not a
farthing over. Doubloons, Louis d'ors and pieces
of eight. Guineas, too. The guineas should do.
Put the rest back. What are you looking for?

JIM

Flint's Fist.

MRS. HAWKINS

What in the world might that be?

JIM

It's a map to find Captain Flint's treasure.

MRS HAWKINS

Captain Flint! The pirate? We don't want
anything to do with pirates.

She pulls Jim away from the chest. A whistle is heard off.

Mercy, now what?

JIM

It must be the signal.

MRS. HAWKINS

Pulling Jim out of the room.

Come on, Jim, quickly, quickly!

*Jim frees himself, runs back to the chest,
pulls out an oilskin packet.*

JIM

This must be it.

*There is a sound of a stick tap-tapping
outside. Jim and Mrs Hawkins freeze.*

They're here already, let's go!

*Jim and Mrs. Hawkins rush out behind the bar as
Blind Pew, Black Dog, Dirk enter through the door.*

PEW

In, in, in!

*The pirates creep up on Billy. They think he
is asleep. They all pounce on him.*

HANDS

He's dead!

PEW

What's that?

BLACK DOG

It's Billy Bones. He's dead.

PEW
Don't talk daft! I was with him not minutes since!
DIRK
Well, he's as dead as a door-nail now!
PEW
Then search him, you shirking lubbers.
One of you look in his sea chest.
HANDS
I'll do it.
PEW
Well, is the chart on him?
BLACK DOG
No, Pew, he's as clean as a whistle!
PEW
It's got to be here somewhere!
HANDS
Pew, they've been here before us!
PEW
Eh?
HANDS
Someone's turned the chest out a'low and aloft!
PEW
But is it there?
HANDS
The money's there.
PEW
To hell with the money. Flint's Fist, I mean!
O'BRIEN
I don't see it there no how.
DIRK
And Bill's been overhauled a'ready. There's nothing left!
PEW
It's these people of the inn — it's that boy, that's
who it is. I wish I had put his eyes out!

BLACK DOG
They were here no time ago.
HANDS
That's right.
PEW
Scatter, lads, and find them!
HANDS
Pointing at lantern
They can't be far; they left their lamp in Bill's room.
PEW
Scatter and find 'em! Rout the house
out. Turn the inn upside-down!
The pirates wreak havoc on the inn. A whistle
is heard off stage, then another whistle.
BLACK DOG
That's Morgan!
MERRY
Twice! We'll have to budge, mates.
PEW
Budge, you skulk! Shiver my soul, if only I had eyes!
DIRK
Get out of the way, Pew.
PEW
You have your hands on thousands, you fools,
and you hang a leg! You'd be as rich as kings if
you could find it, and you know it's here.
HANDS
We're going to get caught!
PEW
Cowards! And I'm to lose my chance for you! Am I to
be a poor, crawling beggar, sponging for rum, when
I might be rolling in a coach? If you had the pluck of
a weevil in a biscuit, you would catch them still.

HANDS

Hang it, Pew, we've got the doubloons!

DIRK

They might have hid the blessed thing.

HANDS

Take the Georges, Pew, and don't stand there squalling.

PEW

Squalling I am, is it? We're not leaving
here till we have Flint's map!

BLACK DOG

But Morgan's signal! There are people coming up the hill.

Pew blocks the exit as we hear horses approaching.

DIRK

Budge, Pew!

Pew lashes out with his stick. It is a swords-
stick which Pew uses with great skill.

Take him, mates!

They overthrow Pew and leave him on
the floor and make their escape.

PEW

Wait, shipmates! You wouldn't leave
me behind, would you? Israel!

DR. LIVESEY

Off stage

Don't let them get away!

Pew crawls and touches Billy.

PEW

Ahhhh! Bill Bones, you've done for us. Mates, don't
leave poor old Pew alone with a dead man.

A shot is heard. Pew crashes around
the room till he finds the exit.

Don't desert old Pew!

He exits. The horses get louder as they approach.

SQUIRE

Off stage

Look out there. Get out of the way!

Gun shot..Pew screams. Silence for a moment. More gun shots are heard. Then Jim runs in, followed by Dr. Livesey and Squire Trelawney Holding up a lamp.

It's lucky for you, young Hawkins, that Livesey and I happened to be in the area.

A voice off stage

One of them's dead, sir, and the rest are running for their lives!

SQUIRE

Shouts to off stage.

Take the men and comb the hedgerows! Seek them out! Hurry, lad! Go on, go on!

Mrs. Hawkins enters.

LIVESEY

Mrs. Hawkins, what's going on here?

MRS. HAWKINS

Pirates, sir!

JIM

They are what's left of Flint's crew, sir, and they were after this,

He holds up the oilskin packet.

Flint's treasure map!

Together.

DR. LIVESEY

You know who Flint was?

You must have heard of him?

SQUIRE

You must have heard of him?

You know who Flint was?

SQUIRE

Heard of him! He was the blood-thirstiest buccaneer that ever sailed. Blackbeard was a child to Flint. If that is indeed

Flint's map, this will lead us to the largest hoard of gold and jewels ever amassed. You know what I'll do? I'll fit out a ship in Bristol dock and take you and Hawkins here along, and we'll have that treasure if we search a year.

DR. LIVESEY

If Jim's agreeable, we'll open this packet.

Jim nods and Dr. Livesey opens the oilskin packet. An old map falls out. Everyone gathers around the table.

Spy-glass shoulder, bearing a point to the North of Northeast, Mizzenmast Hill East by Southeast. Tall Tree, cave... Treasure!

SQUIRE

Treasure, by Jove! Livesey, you will give up your wretched practice at once. Tomorrow, I start for Bristol. In three weeks time...two weeks...ten days...we'll have the best ship, sir, and the choicest crew in all England. Hawkins shall come as cabin-boy and we'll all share in the treasure. And, after what's happened here tonight, I expect you could do with the extra money to repair the inn.

DR. LIVESEY

Squire!

JIM

Can I go, I promise I'll be careful! Squire Trelawney is right, we do need the money. We could buy a new inn!

MRS. HAWKINS

I don't care about the money, Jim.

(Reluctantly)

You just come home safe.

SQUIRE

Then that's agreed. You, Livesey, are a ship's doctor; I am admiral. We'll take Redruth, and Hunter. We'll have favorable winds, a quick passage and not the least difficulty in finding the spot; and money to eat, to roll in, to play duck and drake with ever after.

DR. LIVESEY
I'll go with you, Squire Trelawney, but
there's one man I'm afraid of.
SQUIRE
Who's that? Name the dog, sir.
DR. LIVESEY
You, sir, for you cannot hold your tongue. We are not the
only men who know of this paper. We must none of us
go alone till we get to sea. Jim and I shall stick together
in the meanwhile; you'll take Anderson and Tom Hunter
when you ride to Bristol, and, from first to last, not one
of us must breathe a word of what we've found.
SQUIRE
Livesey, you are always in the right of it. I'll be as silent
as the grave. I'll give you a toast: Treasure Island!
ALL
Treasure Island!
The lights fade down as Jim walks forward into a pin-spot.
CHANTEYMAN
Sings
**SO HEAVE HER UP AND AWAY WE'LL GO,
HOORAW, BOYS, HOORA HO.
NOW DON'T YIZ TELL 'EM ALL YIZ KNOW,
HEAVE AWAY HOORAH FOR A ROLL AND GO.**
JIM
(To audience)
So the weeks passed, till one fine
morning there came a letter.

BRISTOL DOCKS

*A concertina quietly plays a sea chantey. A follow spot
picks up Squire Trelawney, who rides in on one of the
platforms, as if in a boat. Dry ice floods the stage.*

SQUIRE

Dear Livesey. The ship is bought and fitted. You never imagined a sweeter schooner — two hundred tons, name: Hispaniola. I got her through my old friend, Blandy, who is an admirable fellow — literally slaved in my interest — and so, I may say, did everyone in Bristol as soon as they got wind of the port we sailed for — treasure, I mean.

Jim, who is still standing on stage,
watches the scene change.

JIM

Shaking his head

Dr. Livesey will not like that.

SQUIRE

It was the crew that troubled me. I wished for a round score of men — in case of natives, buccaneers or the odious French — and I had a most remarkable stroke of good fortune — I fell in talk with an old sailor called Silver, who keeps a public ale house. He knows all the sea-faring men in Bristol.

Long John Silver arrives on another "boat," which "docks" to take its place in forming the configuration of the Bristol Docks setting. He is sitting on a crate with his legs hidden from view.

He said he had lost his health ashore and wanted a good berth as a cook to get to sea again. I was monstrously touched — so would you have been — and out of pure pity, I engaged him on the spot to be the ship's cook. Well, sir, I thought I had only found a cook, but it was a crew I had discovered. Between Silver and myself we got together a company of the toughest old salts imaginable — not pretty to look at, but fellows, by their faces, of the most indomitable spirit. I declare, we could fight a frigate. So now, Livesey, come posthaste; do not lose an hour. Let young Hawkins go at once to see his mother with Redruth for a guard and then both come full speed to Bristol.

The concertina fades out as the lights dim.

CHANTEYMAN

LIFT HIM UP AND CARRY HIM ALONG,
FIRE MARENGO, FIRE HIM AWAY, HEY.
STOW IN THE HOLD WHERE HE BELONG,
FIRE MARENGO, FIRE HIM AWAY.
EASE HIM IN AND LET HIM LAY,
ONE MORE TURN LADS THEN BELAY.

The crew are loading the Ship with barrels, boxes,
crates, bales, ropes, etc. Silver is surrounded by
Merry, Hands, Dirk, Mr. Arrow and Black Dog.
Dirk is bitten by the PARROT, Cap'n Flint.

PARROT

Who squawks, on tape
Pieces of eight, pieces of eight.

SILVER

Cap'n Flint don't like to be touched.
Don't trust nobody but me.

JIM

Excuse me, sir, I'm looking for a gentleman
by the name of Long John Silver.

SILVER

Well, lad, you need look no further.

JIM

Mr. Silver, sir?

SILVER

Yes, young man, such is my name, to be sure.

JIM

I'm Jim Hawkins.

SILVER

Ah! You must be our new cabin-boy. Pleased I am
to see you. Look, everybody, our new cabin-boy.

Everyone turns to look at Jim. Jim
sees Black Dog and points.

23

JIM

You! That man! Stop him! He's a pirate!

The pirates start to panic

He's Black Dog!

Black Dog runs off. Silver throws his crutch after Black Dog,
then grabs hold of Jim before he can run after Black Dog.

SILVER

A pirate on Bristol dock? Get after him.
What did you say his name was?
Black what?

JIM

Dog, sir. Has Mr. Trelawney not told you of
the buccaneers? He was one of them.

SILVER

Dirk, get after him. One of those swabs, was he?
Black Dog? No, I don't know the name, not I. Yet,
I kind of think I've...yes, I've seen the swab. He
used to come round here with a blind beggar.

JIM

That he did, you may be sure. I knew that
blind man, too. His name was Pew.

SILVER

It was! Pew! That be his name for certain.
Ah, he looked a shark, he did!

DIRK

Dirk returns.

I lost him, Long John. He disappeared in the crowd.

SILVER

Got clean away, did he?

DIRK

Aye, that he did. There are too many people abroad.

Dirk gives Silver back his crutch. Silver stands
up. This is the first time that we see that he
has one leg. Jim reacts. Silver smiles.

SILVER

Dirk, take, cap'n Flint below will yer. See here, now, Hawkins, here's a blessed thing. There's Cap'n Trelawney...what's he to think? Here you comes and tells me of it plain; and here I let him give us all the slip before my blessed deadlights! You're a lad, you are, but you're smart as paint. I seen that when I first saw you. What could I do, with this old timber I hobble on? Shiver my timbers, to think we had a pirate in our midst. You got sharp eyes, lad. You and me should make a good crew. But come now, stand by to go about. Dooty is dooty. We must report this 'ere affair to Cap'n Trelawney. Well, dash my buttons, here he is now.

Livesey and Squire Trelawney meet Silver and Jim mid stage.

SQUIRE

Well, young Hawkins, what do you think of the ship?

JIM

She's wonderful, sir. We've just seen Black Dog.

DR. LIVESEY

Where, Jim?

SILVER

Here on the dock. One of the crew run after him but lost him in the town, today being market day an' all.

DR. LIVESEY

I was afraid something like this would happen.

SQUIRE

We must be on our guard.

SILVER

I feel bad that the villainous swab was a part of our company. I should have been more careful.

SQUIRE

Think no more of it. You weren't to know.

SILVER

Thank you kindly, sir.

SQUIRE

You're a good man, Silver! All hands
aboard by four this afternoon.

SILVER

Aye, aye, sir.

Silver exits.

DR. LIVESEY

Well, Squire, I don't put much faith in your discoveries, as
a general thing; but I will say this, John Silver suits me.

SQUIRE

The man's a perfect trump. Ah! There's Smollett...

CAPTAIN SMOLLETT

*Enters from on board the Hispaniola. He
salutes and starts down the gang plank.*

Squire Trelawney, may I have a word?

SQUIRE

Smollett, I am always at the Captain's orders. What have
you to say? All well, I hope; all shipshape and seaworthy?

SMOLLETT

Well, sir, better speak plain, I believe, even at the risk of
offense. I don't like this cruise, I don't like my first mate
and I don't like the crew. That's short and sweet.

SQUIRE

Perhaps, sir, you don't like the ship?

SMOLLETT

I can't speak as to that, sir, not having seen her tried.

SQUIRE

Possibly, sir, you may not like your employer, either?

DR. LIVESEY

Jumping between them.

Stay a bit, stay a bit. The captain has said too much or he
has said too little, You don't like this cruise. Now, why?

SMOLLETT

I was engaged, sir, on what we call sealed
orders, to sail this ship for that

gentleman where he should bid me. So far, so good.
But now I find that every man before the mast knows
more than I do. It has even been told to the
bloody parrot.
SQUIRE
Silver's parrot?
SMOLLET
I don't call that fair, now, do you?
DR. LIVESEY
Looking at Trelawney
No, I don't.
SMOLLET
I learn we are going after treasure. Now
treasure is tickilish work.I don't like
treasure voyages.
SQUIRE
Wait! Wait! I never told that to a soul!
SMOLLET
The hands know it, sir. I have heard that you have a
map of an island, that there's crosses on the map to
show where treasure is, and that the island lies...
SQUIRE
(Quickly)
Livesey, that must have been you or young Hawkins!
DR. LIVESEY
It doesn't much matter who it was now. Next, you say
you don't like the crew. Are they not good seamen?
SMOLLETT
I don't like them, sir.
DR. LIVESEY
Then tell us what you want us to do..
SMOLLETT
Well, gentlemen, are you determined to go on this cruise?
SQUIRE
Like iron.

LIVESEY
Yes
SMOLLETT
Very good. I suggest, for your safety's sake, and for
your security, that you put the powder and arms in your
own cabin with you. First point.Then I hear that you are
bringing two of your own people along with you. Why
not give them the cabin next to yours. Second point.
SQUIRE
Any more?
SMOLLETT
One more; there's been too much blabbing already.
DR. LIVESEY
Far too much.
SMOLLETT
Well, gentlemen, I don't know who has this map,
but I make it a point — it shall be kept secret,
DR. LIVESEY
I see. You wish us to keep this matter dark and to make
a garrison of the stern part of the ship, manned with my
friend's own people and provided with all the arms and
powder on board. In other words, you fear a mutiny.
SMOLLETT
No captain, sir, would be justified in going to sea
at all if he had grounds enough to say that.
DR. LIVESEY
Captain Smollett, you'll excuse me. When you came here,
I'll stake my wig, you meant to say more than this?
SMOLLETT
When I came here I meant to get discharged. I had
no thought that Mr.Trelawney would hear a word.
SQUIRE
No more I would. Had Livesey not been here, I should
have seen you to the deuce. As it is, I have heard you.
I will do as you desire, but I think the worse of you.

SMOLLETT

That's as you please, sir. You'll find I do my duty.

Smollett turns and goes back up the gangplank.

LIVESEY

Trelawney, contrary to all my notions, I believe
you have managed to get two honest men on
board with you — that man and John Silver.

SQUIRE

Silver, if you like, but as for that intolerable
humbug, I declare I think his conduct unmanly,
unsailorly and downright un-English!

DR. LIVESEY

Well, we shall see. Jim, would you like to go aboard now?

JIM

Oh, yes, please, sir!

SQUIRE

Then let us do so.

CHANTEYMAN

Sings

**SO HEAVE HER UP AND AWAY WE'LL GO HOORAW,
BOYS HOORAW HO....**

*They make their way up the gangplank. Silver enters
with his parrot in a cage. Anderson enters with muskets.
As soon as* Silver gets *aboard, he goes to Mr Arrow.*

SILVER

So ho, mates, and Mr. Arrow! What's all this?

ARROW

We're a-changing of the powder, Long John.

SILVER

What! Why, by the powers, if we do we'll miss the tide!

SMOLLETT

Coming forward

The crew will be wanting supper.

SILVER

Aye, aye, sir.

Silver goes below. Jim walks up to Smollett and smiles.

SMOLLETT

And as for you, ship's boy, there's work to be done. Splice the end of this rope. I'll have no favorites on my ship.

JIM

Aye, aye, Captain!

Jim looks at the rope, not knowing what to do.

CHANTEYMAN

Sings

HEAVE HER UP.......

The lights fade.

HISPANIOLA

The Hispaniola is created in front of the audience. A major piece of theater craft involving ropes, ratlings. masts, platforms, barrels, sails and wind.Using the ropes that are hanging down; they become the mooring ropes, the sail ropes. A barrel becomes the capstan and oars crossed, become the levers.The ships wheel sits on one of the platforms. A silk sheet becomes the sail.Wind, a fan.As the various tasks are performed they are accompanied by sea chanteys.

SMOLLETT

Mr. Arrow, get us underway.

ARROW

Aye, sir. Helm over hard to larboard!

MERRY

Hard to larboard, aye.

CHANTEYMAN

Sings a sea chantey medley.

HANG DOWN YOUR BLOOD RED ROSES.

ARROW

Brace the fore and foretop! Sharp to larboard! Standby the main sheets!

CHANTEYMAN

Sings

LITTLE NELLY SKINNER

The main sail drops in.

ARROW

Take in the bow, stern and spring lines!

DIRK

Bow line, aye.

MORGAN

Stern line, aye.

O'BRIEN

Spring line, aye.

ARROW

Hold fast the stern spring and wait my command!

CHANTEYMAN

Sings

HAUL ON THE BOWLINE.

Jim bumps into Mr. Arrow, who throws him to the deck.

REDRUTH

Picking him up

You stay with me, Master Jim.

ARROW

Let go the stern spring line! Haul the main sheets!

MORGAN

Stern spring line, aye. Man the capstan.

CHANTEYMAN

Sings

ROLLICKING RANDY DANDY OH!

ARROW

Captain, free and clear! Helm come quarter Sou', Sou' west!

MERRY

Quarter Sou', Sou, west, aye.

The sails above the audience and on the mast fill with wind.

CHANTEYMAN

Sings

WALK HIM ALONG

JIM

To the audience, as a spot comes up on him. He is working on the splice.

I'm not going to relate the voyage in detail. The ship proved to be a good ship, and Captain Smollett thoroughly understood his business. As for Mr. Arrow, he turned out even worse than the captain had feared. He had no command among the men. And after a day or two at sea, he began to appear on deck drunk. Time after time he was ordered below in disgrace. In the meantime, we could never make out where he got his drink.

ARROW

We'll have no lazy landlubbers on this ship, even if you are a friend of that loose-tongued squire. Did you finish the splice that the captain asked you for?

JIM

I have no idea how to do it, sir.

ARROW

Grabbing Jim.

You address me as "Mr. Arrow!" when you speak to me.

JIM

Yes, sir.

Mr. Arrow strikes Jim with his belt several times.

ARROW

You insolent whelp!

He goes to hit Jim again.

I told you: Mr. Arrow.

Silver enters with his parrot and carrying a bucket.

SILVER

Easy, easy, Mr. Arrow. Leave the boy alone.
*Mr. Arrow looks at Silver, and backs down
and exits muttering. Jim is devastated. Sits
with his head in his hands. Silver sits.*
Jolly little soul is our Mr. Arrow, ain't 'e?
Jim looks up and smiles.
Come away, Hawkins. Come and have a yarn with
Long John. I'll show you what to do with that.
Silver takes Jim's rope and throws it overboard.

JIM

(Shocked)
What did you do that for?

SILVER

This is just between you and me. We all
needs a bit of help now and then.
Silver winks at Jim and hands him a spliced piece of rope.
Here's Cap'n Flint predicting success to our voyage.
To the parrot
Wasn't you, Cap'n? What's that, Cap'n?
He draws a knife and points it at Jim.
Peel spuds? Right you are, Cap'n. Here, lad, give us a hand.

PARROT

On tape
Pieces of eight! Pieces of eight! Pieces of eight!

SILVER

Now, that there bird is maybe two hundred years old,
Hawkins. They lives forever mostly; and if anybody's
seen more wickedness, it must be the devil himself.

PARROT

On tape
Stand by to go about!

SILVER

Ah, she's a handsome craft, she is.

PARROT
On tape
Land lubbers is swabs!
SILVER
You can't touch pitch and not be mucked, lad. Here's this poor, old, innocent bird o'mine swearing blue fire, and none the wiser, you may lay to that.
PARROT
On tape
Land lubbers is swabs!
SILVER
She would swear the same, in a manner of speaking, before a chaplain.
JIM
Were you ever a land lubber, Long John?
SILVER
Aye, lad. I had good schooling in my younger days, Jim. I could have amounted to a deal more than I am today. I tell you, if I hadn't lost my old leg in the service of the King —God bless him — maybe I would have become...
JIM
A lord in Parliament?
SILVER
Aye, lad! Right you are. Riding in a coach with a fat pension and all, and here I am among this pack of sea dogs. How you getting on with those spuds? Looks to me as if you are a dab hand with a knife.
Jim holds out his hand and Cap'n Flint climbs up his arm. Silver is taken aback.
SILVER
Well, dang me! I ain't never seen the likes of that before. Cap'n Flint seems to have taken a real shine to you. Always said that bird had good taste.
Distant thunder
I think we may be in for a bit of nasty weather.

Closer thunder

Jim, me lad, stow Cap'n Flint below for me, will you, matey?
*As Jim goes below, a very drunken Mr. Arrow
enters and lumbers towards Silver. The
stage darkens. A storm is brewing.*

You be stinking again, Mr. Arrow, and no mistake

ARROW

Watch your bilge, Silver... I only need a little
more to set me right in me berth.

SILVER

(Furious)

Damn you for a river rat...

ARROW

Belay, John Silver! Give me what I need!
Give it now! Or else I.......

*Silver looks to see if the coast is clear, then produces the
silver brandy flask, "Little Davy Jones," from inside his jacket.
Arrow snatches the flask, puts it to his lips and starts to drink.*

SILVER

Curse you for a damn fool.

Silver takes the flask back from Arrow.

ARROW

Snatching it back

I need more!

SILVER

Then drink to the devil!

Arrow drains the flask dry and throws it back to Silver.

STORM

SMOLLET

All hands on deck!

ARROW

All hands on deck!

*The storm intensifies. Everybody comes on deck
to fight the storm. During this action, Silver saves*

Jim's life as a big wave hits the deck,(in the form of a blue silk). Mr. Arrow is swept overboard.
SILVER
Looking at the flask
Man Overboard!!!
CHANTEYMAN
(On tape)
WE'LL PITCH HIM DOWN IN THE DEEP DARK HOLE.
YO, HO, HO, AND A BOTTLE OF RUM.
WHERE THE SHARKS 'LL HAVE HIS BODY
AND THE DEVIL TAKE HIS SOUL,
INTO YO, HO, HO, HUM.
The storm slowly subsides.

BELOW DECKS

JIM
To the audience
With Mr. Arrow gone, every man on
board seemed much happier.
The food for the crew was awful. So, to vary their diet,
Squire Trelawney had a barrel of apples placed on the
lower deck for everyone to help himself that had a fancy.
If it had not been for that apple barrel, we would not
have had warning of the treachery about to befall us.
*He reaches in, but, because the barrel is almost
empty, he tips it over and crawls inside to get an
apple.At this moment, Silver and Dirk enters.*
DIRK
Was you Flint's first mate, Long John?
SILVER
No, no, you got it wrong. I was Flint's quartermaster,
along of my timber leg. The same broadside I
lost my leg, old Pew lost his deadlights.

DIRK

Ah! But, Flint was the flower of the flock!

SILVER

I laid two thousand safe from Flint and nine
hundred from Cap'n England. That ain't bad for a
man before the mast — all safe in the bank.

Hands, Morgan, Merry and O'Brien enter.

MORGAN

Long John, I'm starving hungry!

SILVER

Get I'm an apple Dirk.

*Dirk starts to reach in to get the apple but
Merry Intercepts him.*

MERRY

When are we going to get some decent grub?

HANDS

Look here, this is what I want to know, John, how long
are we a-going to stand off like a blessed bum boat?

SILVER

Israel, your head ain't much account, nor ever was. But
you're able to hear, I reckon; least ways, your ears is big
enough. You'll berth forward and you'll live hard and you'll
speak soft and you'll keep sober till I give the word.

HANDS

Well, I don't say no, do I? What I say
is, when? That's what I say.

SILVER

I'll tell you when! When I know for certain who is joining
us. Then, at the very last moment, that's when! Here's a
first-rate seaman, Cap'n Smollett, sails the blessed ship
for us. Here's this squire and doctor with a map and such,
I don't know where it is, do I? No more do you, you says.
Well then, this squire and doctor shall find the stuff and help
us get it aboard, by the powers. Then we'll see. If I was

sure of you all, sons of double Dutchmen, I'd have Cap'n
Smollett navigate us half-way back again before I struck.
DIRK
Why, we're all seamen aboard here, I should think.
SILVER
We're all foc's'le hands, you mean. We can
steer a course, but who's to set one?
HANDS
Easy all, Long John. Who's a-crossin' of you?
DIRK
But, when we do lay 'em athwart, what
are we to do with them anyhow?

SILVER
There's the man for me! That's what I call business. Dooty
is dooty, mates. I give you my vote — death. Dead men
don't bite. But wait is what I say; we'll finish with 'em at the
island, as soon's the treasure's on board, and a pity it is.
HANDS
John, you're our man!
*The ship lurches and the barrel travels across the
space. Dirk goes towards the barreled and with
Merry without looking set the barrel upright.*
MERRY
Wait! This is all very well for you, Silver, snug
in your galley, but I've had my fill of Smollet
treating me like a slave. I say now!
MORGAN
George is right. Do it now. I'm so hungry that my
stomach feels that my throat's been cut.
DIRK
Me, too. Only one thing I claim — I claim Trelawney. I'll
wring his calf's head off his body with these hands.
Pirates agree

SILVER

Alright, lads, you win, have it your own way. But I warned
you, so don't come squalling to me later. Now, Dirk, jump up
like a sweet lad and get me an apple to wet my pipe like.

*Dirk takes out a knife to stab an apple in the
barrel Just as he is about to stab.....*

Off stage

Land ho!

CHANTEYMAN

Sings

LOWLANDS LOW.......

*Pirates exit. A very frightened Jim climbs
out of the apple barrel. On the
cyclorama we see the silhouette of Treasure
Island growing out of the mist.*

DECK HISPANIOLA

*Everybody now comes up on deck. They all make their way
to the ship's rail, Silver and his mates being the first there.
The ship tacks. The scene is now played downstage.*

SMOLLETT

Hard to larboard.

MERRY

Hard to larboard, aye, aye, Sir.

SMOLLET

Has any one of you ever seen that land ahead?

SILVER

I have, Sir I've watered there with a trader I was cook in.

SMOLLETT

The anchorage is on the South, behind an islet, I fancy?

SILVER

(Overly eager.)

Yes, sir, Skeleton Island they calls it. It
were a main place for pirates once.

(Realizing he has said too much.)
A hand we had on board knowed all their names for
it. That hill to the Nor'ard they calls the Fore-mast
Hill, but the main — that's the big 'un with the cloud
on it — they usually calls the Spy-glass, by reason of
a lookout they kept when they was in the anchorage
cleaning, for it's there they cleaned their ships, sir.
SMOLLETT
I have a chart here. See if that's the place.
Smollett hands Silver a map, a "copy" of the treasure map.
SILVER
Yes, sir, this is the spot, and very prettily drawed
out. Aye, here it is: "Cap'n Kidd's Anchorage"
— just the name my shipmate called it.
SMOLLETT
Thank you, my man. I'll ask you later on to give us a help.
SILVER
I'd be happy to, sir.
SMOLLETT
You may go.
SILVER
Thank you, sir.
Jim runs to Dr. Livesey. He pulls the doctor aside.
JIM
Doctor, may I speak? Can you get the captain
and the squire down to the cabin? Make some
pretense to send for me. I have terrible news!
(Livesey glances around. He sees Silver.)
DR. LIVESEY
Thank you, Jim
Loudly for the sake of the pirates.
That was all I wanted to know.
*Livesey walks back to Smollett and
they talk together as they exit.*

SILVER

Ah, Jim, this here is a sweet spot, this island, a sweet spot for a lad to go ashore on. You'll bathe, you'll climb trees and you'll hunt goats, you will. It's a pleasant thing to be young and have ten toes, you may lay to that. When you want to do a bit of exploring, you just ask old John and he'll put up a snack for you to take along.

REDRUTH

Master Hawkins, you are wanted below in the cabin.

JIM

(With great relief)

Thank you, Redruth.

Jim exchanges a look with Silver.

CAPTAIN'S CABIN

Dr. Livesey, Squire Trelawney, Redruth and Captain Smollett and Jim are in conversation

LIVESEY

So that's the way the wind blows. Well done, Jim.

JIM

Thank you, sir.

SQUIRE

Well, Smollett, it seems I owe you an apology. You were right and I was wrong. I own myself an ass.

LIVESEY

Silver is a very remarkable man.

SMOLLETT

He'll look remarkably well from a yard-arm, sir. He has fooled all of us, but that's as maybe. I see three or four points, and with Mr. Trelawney's permission, I'll name them.

SQUIRE

(Grandly)

You, sir, are the captain. It is for you to speak.

SMOLLETT

Point one... We must go on, because we can't turn back. If I gave the word to go about, they would rise at once. Point two... We now know what they intend to do. We have time before us — at least until the treasure's found. Point three... There are faithful hands. We can count, I take it, on your own home servants, Mr. Trelawney?

SQUIRE

As upon myself.

REDRUTH

Aye, sir, you can.

SMOLLETT

Now, who else is there? Tom Hunter and Alan — and Israel Hands of course.

JIM

No, he's with Silver.

SQUIRE

Hands with Silver? I recruited Hands myself... on Silver's recommendation, of course.

SMOLLETT

I did think I could have trusted Hands!

SQUIRE

And to think that they're all Englishmen! Sir, I could find it in my heart to blow up the ship.

SMOLLETT

Opens the map

That's as may be Squire but, this ship needs to take on provisions and water, without which she cannot sail. There is only one place on the island for fresh water and that is by the stockade that Flint built. If we could get our arms and supplies to the stockade, we could hold off an army.

DR. LIVESEY

You should put that chart in a safe place, Captain.

SMOLLETT

Folding map

Don't worry, sir, this is a copy without the fine details, if you take my meaning. The real chart is safe and sound.

There is a knock at the cabin door.

SQUIRE

Who is it?

REDRUTH

Off stage

It's Redruth, sir.

Redruth enters the cabin.

I'm sorry, sir, but there's trouble with the crew.

SQUIRE

It's started already!

SMOLLETT

To Redruth

Go on, man.

ANDERSON

There's going to be a mutiny. Silver is trying to hold the men back, but they want the chart of the island.

SMOLLETT

Then, by Saint George, they shall have it.

He whispers to Redruth who exits. Smollet opens the map.

Now, where shall I mark the treasure?

He picks up a quill and makes a cross on the map.

There, Flint's treasure!

There is a commotion outside.

DR. LIVESEY

Arm yourselves, gentlemen, I believe
we are due for a visitation.

*The cabin door bursts open and Silver and
the crew enter, including Tom Hunter.*

SMOLLETT

What is the meaning of this?

SILVER

It's a sort of deputation, sir.

SMOLLETT

A deputation, is it?

SQUIRE

What do you want?

SILVER

The men here have been hearing
stories about this here island.

SMOLLETT

What sort of stories?

TOM

That there be buried treasure.

CREW

That's right, treasure! Buried treasure!

SQUIRE

Don't be ridiculous. Who told you such a thing?

TOM

Why, you did, Squire.

SQUIRE

What!... Well, I....Tom Hunter — out of all the men
in my employ, I thought you could be trusted.

SILVER

Now, treasure to these men is like a carrot to a
donkey. They want to get their hands on it.

SMOLLETT

So, this is mutiny?

SILVER

No! Well, yes, you could put it like that, sir.

SMOLLETT

I'll see you all hang from the yard-arm!

SILVER

I have negotiated fair terms for your safety.

SQUIRE

What on earth do you mean?

SILVER

You have a chart of the island.

CREW

Aye! Flint's Fist! Flint's map!

SMOLLETT

Well?

SILVER

We want it.

CREW

Aye, give us the map!

SMOLLETT

All right. Suppose I give you this chart.
What then happens to us?

SILVER

Well...nothing, Cap'n.

DR. LIVESEY

You'll not harm us in any way?

SILVER

You have my word, gentlemen!

SQUIRE

Indicating the crew

What about them?

SILVER

I speak for them as well.

SMOLLETT

Very well, as long as I have your solemn
promise. Here is the map.

He throws map down

O'BRIEN

Moving in.

Come on, mates, over the side with them!

CREW

Aye! Make them walk the plank! Feed 'em to the fishes!

SILVER

Back, back!

45

SMOLLETT
Drawing his pistol
So much for your promise, Silver! Get back or
I'll blast one of you to kingdom come.
SILVER
Get back, you swabs.
MORGAN
We got the map. Let's do for them!
CREW
Aye, do for 'em!
SILVER
Yes, we got the map, by thunder, but we got it too easy.
HANDS
What do you mean?
DIRK
You think it's a trick?
SILVER
There's only one way to find out. We'll go ashore
and see. But just to be on the safe side, we'll
take young Hawkins with us as a hostage.
He grabs hold of Jim.
LIVESEY
God help you, Silver, if you harm a hair of his head!
JIM
I'm not afraid, Sir!
SILVER
Now, Hands and O'Brien, stay here and keep
these gentlemen company. At the first sign of any
trouble...you fire, and the shot will signal young
Hawkins' execution! Now, lower a boat.
CHANTEYMAN
Sings
LOWLANDS [SECOND VERSE]
*They all leave the cabin and make their way to
the deck. A boat is lowered over the side.*

SILVER

In, in, young Hawkins.

Jim, Silver and the crew climb over the side.
Everyone else watches from the rail. Off stage

Pull, you swabs; pull for the shore!

MERRY

The treasure's good as ours, ain't it, John?

DIRK

Aye, it's ours for the taking of!

SILVER

We shall see. Now pull for the shore. Pull, you swabs!

The pirates race for the shore. Smollett,
Trelawney and Dr. Livesey watch them go.

ON DECK

SQUIRE

Pointing

They're making for that little cove.

SMOLLETT

It'll be difficult for them to land there. There's no beach.

DR. LIVESEY

You're right. The undergrowth is right to the
water's edge. They'll never get through it.

SQUIRE

Is that young Hawkins standing up in the bow?

SMOLLETT

He's grabbed a branch of a tree! He's out of the boat.

DR. LIVESEY

He's off into the woods like a hare!

SQUIRE

Great Scot, he's got clean away!

Redruth surreptitiously enters with a musket.
He confronts Hands and O'Brien.

47

REDRUTH

One move, and you are dead men!

HANDS

What the devil...?

REDRUTH

Up with your hands. Keep your hands in the air.

SQUIRE

Well done, man!

SMOLLETT

Take their weapons away.

REDRUTH

At once, sir.

O'BRIEN

You won't get away with this!

SMOLLETT

Stow them below and make sure they can't escape.

REDRUTH

Aye, aye, Sir.

DR. LIVESEY

You have a plan, Captain?

SMOLLETT

I have, sir. Gentlemen, help me lower another boat.

SQUIRE

Where are we going?

SMOLLETT

To the only safe place on the island. Flint's stockade! From there, with luck, we might be able to rescue young Hawkins.

Anderson exits with Hands and O'Brien.

Come, gentlemen, to the boats.

.Ad lib "put your shoulder to it" etc.

There is a sound of splintering wood, then Hands and O'Brien enter up from below decks.

REDRUTH

off stage

Stay where you are!

Sounds of crashing.Redruth Runs on.

I couldn't hold em, Sir.

SMOLLET

Give me those pistols. All of you get in the boat. Go !Go!

*The boat pulls away. Israel and O'Briens head's
appear round a corner. Smollet fires the two pistols
grabs a rope and swings onto the departing boat.*

That should hold them. Come, gentlemen,
let us rescue young Hawkins.

O'BRIEN

Entering

There they be now! Rowing like the devil!

HANDS

Don't stand there like a dainty milkmaid,
help me man the cannon!

SMOLLETT

They're aiming the cannon at us!

SQUIRE

Good Heavens! They'll blow us out of the water!

Hands and O'Brien now have the cannon loaded.

SMOLLETT

Row for your lives!

Hands takes the flint stock and lights the cannon.

O'BRIEN

Fire!

*The cannon goes off with an earsplitting crash. We hear the
cannonball scream across the stage and, just before it hits
the water, we go to black. We hear the cannon ball splash
into the water. Half the audience should feel the spray.*

End of Act 1

ACT TWO

SKELETON ISLAND

*Noises of startled island creatures. Jim runs
on, looking for somewhere to hide.*
SILVER
Shouting
Jim! Jim, can you hear me?
Jim hides as Tom and Silver enter.
TOM
We'll never find him.
SILVER
Sure we will!
TOM
Silver I have changed my mind!
SILVER
Wipes his face
It's hot! Look, mate, it's because I thinks gold dust of
you, gold dust. And you may lay to that! If I hadn't took
to you like pitch, do you think I'd have been here
a-warning of you? All's up — you can't make nor mend.
TOM
I draw the line at murder.
SILVER
It's to save your neck that I'm a-speaking of. If one of them
wild 'uns heard me, where'd I be, Tom, where'd I be?
TOM
Silver, you're old, but you're brave or I'm mistook.
And will you let yourself be led away with that mess
of swabs? Not you! As sure as God sees me, I'd
sooner lose my hand than turn to killing.
*There is a blood-curdling scream in the
distance. Tom and Silver look off.*
What in heavens name was that?

SILVER

That would be young Alan, I reckon; he
never could make up his mind!

TOM

(Shocked)

Alan? Then rest his soul for a true seaman! As for you, John
Silver, long you've been a mate of mine, but you're a mate of
mine no more. If I die like a dog, I'll die in my dooty. You've
killed Alan, have you? Then kill me, too, if you can. But I
defies you.

Tom turns to leave.

SILVER

Settle down now, Tom. I'm sure we can work all this out.
Have a drink out of little Davy Jones to show there's no
hard feelings. You and me is like two peas in a pod.

*Silver reaches inside his jacket and pulls out the brandy
flask. As Tom drinks, Silver swings his crutch and knocks
Tom down. In a flash, Silver is on him, stabbing him until
he stops moving. Silver gets up and hobbles off. Jim enters
slowly and looks at Tom's body.We hear off stage…*

Jim, where are you?

Jim runs out.The Pirates collect Tom's body.

ANOTHER PART OF THE ISLAND

*Jim runs in scared, stops and is aware that he is being
watched. A figure darts from one hiding place to another.
It is BEN GUNN, who finally throws himself to the
ground in front of Jim. Or descends from the ceiling.*

JIM

(Frightened)

Who are you? What do you want?

BEN
(In faulting tones)
Ben Gunn... I'm poor Ben Gunn, I am. I haven't
spoke with a human soul these last three years.

JIM
Three years?

BEN
Aye, three years!

JIM
Were you shipwrecked?

BEN
Nay, mate, marooned.

JIM
You mean, you were left here on purpose...left to die?

BEN
Aye, lad. And lived on goats since then, and berries, and
oysters, but, mate, my heart is sore for a Christian diet.
You mightn't happen to have a piece of cheese about you,
now? No? Many's the night I've dreamed of cheese —
toasted, mostly — and woke up again, and here I were.

JIM
If ever I can get aboard again, you shall
have cheese by the pound.

BEN
If ever you can get aboard again, says you?
Why, now, who's to hinder you?

JIM
Not you, I know.

BEN
And right you was. Now you — what
do you call yourself, mate?

JIM
Jim,

BEN

Jim?Jim! Jim, it were providence that put me here.
I've thought it all out in this here lonely island.
(In a whisper)
I'll tell you what, I'll make a gen'lemen of you, Jim. Ah, Jim,
you'll bless your stars, you will, you was the first that found
me! Now, Jim, you tell me true: that ain't Flint's ship?

JIM

It's not Flint's ship, and Flint is dead; but there
are some of Flint's hands aboard.

BEN

Not a man with...one leg?

JIM

Silver?

BEN

Ah, Silver! That were the name.

JIM

He's the cook, and the ringleader, too.
Ben holds Jim by the wrist.

BEN

If you was sent by Long John, I'm as
good as pork, and I know it.

JIM

Silver didn't send me; in fact I'm running away from him now.
He and Flint's crew mutinied on us. We have Flint's map.

BEN

Flint's Fist? How did you come by that?

JIM

An old seaman called Billy Bones.

BEN

Dead?

JIM

Nods

Dead. I gave the map to the squire, but somehow
Silver and his men heard about it. Early this morning

they mutinied, taking me as a hostage, but I escaped.
Now I need to get back to the Hispaniola.

BEN

Pats Jim on the head.

You're all in a clove hitch, ain't you? Well, you just
put your trust in Ben Gunn. Ben Gunn's the man to
do it. Would you think it likely, now, that your squire
would prove a liberal minded one in case of help,
him being in a clove hitch, as you remark?

JIM

I'm sure he would.

BEN

I didn't mean giving me a job. What I mean is, would he be
likely to come down to the toon of, say, one thousand pounds
out of money that's as good as a man's own already?

JIM

Of course. All hands were to share anyway.

BEN

And a passage home?

JIM

Why, the squire's a gentleman. And besides, if we got rid of
the others, we should want you to help work the vessel home.

Ben leads Jim to a small rock and they both sit.

BEN GUNN

Ah, well! I were in Flint's ship when he buried the treasure.
Six went ashore; only Flint returned. Ah, he was a man,
was Flint! He were afraid of none, not he, Well, I was in
another ship three years back and we sighted this island.
"Boys," said I, "here's Flint's treasure; let's land and find it."
Twelve days they looked for it, and every day they had a
worse word for me, until one fine morning all hands went
aboard. "As for you, Benjamin Gunn," says they, "here's a
musket and a spade and pick-axe. You can stay here and
find Flint's money for yourself," they says. Well, Jim, three

years have I been marooned here. Do I look like a man before the mast? No, says you. Nor I weren't, neither, I says.

He winks at Jim and pinches him.

JIM

Ouch!

BEN GUNN

Just you tell them words to the squire. Three years he were the man of this island and sometimes he would maybe think upon a prayer, and sometimes he would think of his old mother, but most time was taken up in another matter. Then you'll give him a nip, like I do.

Ben pinches Jim again.

JIM

Ouch!

BEN

Gunn is a good man, you'll say, and he puts a precious value — a precious value, mind that— on the word of a gen'leman-born over these gen'lemen of fortune, having been one hisself.

JIM

Well, I'm afraid I don't understand a word of what you've been saying. But that's neither here or there, for how am I to get back on board?

BEN

Ah, that's the hitch, for sure. Well, there's my boat, that I made with my two hands.

Ben shows Jim the boat.

If the worst come to the worst, we might try that after dark.

A cannon is heard in the distance. Ben and Jim both jump. They rush to the side of the stage and look off. A volley of small arms fire is heard.

BEN

Now, there's your friends, sure enough. In the old stockade.

JIM

Far more likely, it's the mutineers.

BEN
Look at the flag! It's the Union Jack!
Silver would fly the Jolly Roger.

JIM
All the more reason that I should join my friends
BEN
You're a good boy, or I'm mistook, but you're on'y a boy,
all told. Now, Ben Gunn is fly. Rum wouldn't bring me
there, where you're going — not rum wouldn't — till I see
your born gen'lemen and gets it on his word of honor.
And you won't forget my words: "A precious value," that's
what you'll say, a precious value — and then nips him.
Ben gives Jim another pinch.
And when Ben Gunn is wanted, you know where to find him,
Jim. And him that comes is to have a white thing in his hand.
JIM
Well, I believe I understand. You have something
to propose, and you wish to see the squire or the
doctor, and you're to be found where I found you.
BEN
You won't forget — precious value?
JIM
Good, and now may I go?
BEN
You won't forget? Precious value. Well, then, I
reckon you can go, Jim. And, Jim, if you was to see
Silver, you wouldn't go for to sell Ben Gunn? Wild
horses wouldn't draw it from you? No, says you.
*Another cannon shot, much nearer
this time. Jim and Ben duck.*
BEN
Good luck, lad.

CHANTEYMAN
Sings
WE'RE FROM THE WALRUS.
Jim takes off through the trees.The lights cross-fade.
The platforms that will create the stockade come
hurtling in, propelled by Livesey and Redruth. Squire
and Smollet are riding on them, firing at the pirates.

THE STOCKADE

From inside the now-formed stockade, Squire, Captain
Smollett, Redruth are shooting into the wings. (Reloading)
SMOLLETT
Keep at it, men. Keep them at bay!
Reloading
We can hold them off here. It's the cannon
fire from the ship that worries me.
REDRUTH
Reloading
That's Israel Hands. Did you know he
was a gunner on Flint's ship?
SMOLLETT
We're out of range here!
A shot from the cannon lands just short of the stockade.
SQUIRE
I hope you are right, Captain!
REDRUTH
Reloading
I think I got one, sir!
SMOLLETT
Well done, Redruth, keep it up.
SQUIRE
I've got another blighter!
SMOLLETT
We'll beat them yet.

DR. LIVESEY
Look, look! They're retreating!
SQUIRE
By Jove, we've got them on the run.
Another cannon shot lands near the stockade.
SQUIRE
Shouting at the ship
Oho! Blaze away!
DR. LIVESEY
Captain, the stockade is quite invisible from the
ship. It must be the flag they were aiming at..
SQUIRE
Would it be wiser to take it down?
SMOLLETT
Strike my colors? No, sir, not I!
REDRUTH
Captain, Captain! We're being hailed!
SQUIRE
Somebody hailing us?
SMOLLETT
Keep your heads down!
REDRUTH
They are waving a white flag, sir!
SQUIRE
Are they indeed?
DR. LIVESEY
It may be a trick.
SILVER
Off stage
Flag of truce!
SMOLLETT
Who goes there? Stand, or we fire.
SILVER
Off stage
Flag of truce, sir.

SMOLLETT

Keep hidden, men. Ten to one this is a trick.

To Silver

And what do you want with your flag of truce?

SILVER

Off stage

Cap'n Silver, Sir, to come aboard and make terms.

Silver enters, waving a white flag.

SMOLLETT

Cap'n Silver! Don't know him. Who's he?

SILVER

Me, Sir. These poor lads have chosen me
Cap'n, after your desertion, Sir.

SMOLLETT

My man, I have not the slightest desire to talk to you,
but if you wish to talk to me, you may approach.

SILVER

That's good enough, Cap'n. A word from you's
enough. I know a gentleman, and you may lay to that...
You ain't a-going to let me into the log-cabin?

SMOLLETT

You can sit on the ground!

SILVER

So be it.

SMOLLETT

Why, Silver, if you had pleased to be an honest man,
you might have been sitting in your galley. It's your own
doing. You're either my ship's cook — and then you
were treated handsome — or Cap'n Silver, a common
mutineer and pirate, and then you can go hang!

SQUIRE

(Fishing for information)

How is the cabin-boy, young Hawkins?

SILVER

Well, enough, when I last saw him.

DR. LIVESEY
If any harm comes to him, so help me...
SMOLLETT
Gentlemen, your posts!
SILVER
Sits down on the ground.
Well, Cap'n, you'll have to give me a hand up again.
A sweet pretty place you have of it here. Why, it's
like a happy family, in a manner of speaking.
SMOLLETT
If you have anything to say, my man, you'd better say it!
SILVER
Right you were, Cap'n Smollett. Dooty is dooty. Well
now, you look here, that was a good trick you played
on us with that chart. We want that treasure and we'll
have it! You would just as soon save your lives, I
reckon. Now, you have the real chart, haven't you?
SMOLLETT
That's as maybe.
SILVER
Ah, well, you have, I know that. You needn't be so
husky with a man. What I mean is, we want your
chart. Now, I never meant you no harm, myself.
SMOLLETT
That won't do with me, my man. We know
exactly what you meant to do, and we don't
care, for now you see, you can't do it.
SILVER
Now, now. You give us the chart to get the treasure by and
we'll offer you a choice. Either you come aboard along of us,
once the treasure is shipped, and then I'll give you my affy-
davy, upon my word of honor, to clap you somewhere safe
ashore. Or, if that ain't to your fancy, then you can stay here,
you can. We'll divide stores with you man for man; and I'll
give my affy-davy, as before, to speak to the first ship I sight

61

and send them here to pick you up. Now, you'll own that's talking. And I hope that all hands in this here stockade will overhaul my words, for what I spoke to one is spoke to all.

SMOLLETT

Is that all?

SILVER

Every last word, by thunder! Refuse that, and you've seen the last of me but musket-balls.

SMOLLETT

Very well. Now you'll hear me. If you'll come up one by one, unarmed, I'll engage to clap you in irons and take you home to a fair trial in England. If you won't, I'll see you all to Davy Jones. You can't find the treasure. You can't sail the ship. Master Silver, you're on a lee shore, and so you'll find out. Those are the last good words you'll get from me, for in the name of heaven, I'll put a bullet in you when next we meet. Tramp, my lad. Bundle out of this place, and double quick!

SILVER

Give me a hand up!

SMOLLETT

Not I.

SILVER

Looking around.

Who'll give me a hand up?

No one moves to help him.

CHANTEYMAN

Sings

BLOW HIGH BLOW LOW AND SO SAILED WE;
FOR I AM A SALT SEA PIRATE
JUST LOOKING FOR A FEE.

Silver crawls along the ground and gets hold of the porch-post to haul himself up. Then with fury he looks about and spits.

SILVER

There! That's what I think of ye. Before an hour's out, I'll stove in your log-house like a rum puncheon. Laugh, by thunder, laugh! Before an hour's out, ye'll laugh on the other side. Them that'll die'll will be the lucky ones!

CHANTEYMAN

Silver climbs over the stockade and is gone.

SMOLLETT

My lads, I've given Silver a broadside. I pitched it in red-hot on purpose, and before long we shall be boarded. We're outnumbered, I needn't tell you that, but we fight in shelter and I've no manner of doubt that we can beat them. To your firing positions, men. Only fire when you know you have a good target. *They all go to their firing positions There is scurrying off stage as the pirates position themselves for attack. Anderson fires off a shot.* Did you hit your man?

REDRUTH

I'm not sure sir...Look out. there's another!

JIM

Off stage

Don't shoot, it's me.

SMOLLET AND DR. LIVESEY

What? Jim!

JIM

Off stage.

Captain Smollett, Squire, Dr. Livesey... Don't shoot!

Jim enters.

SQUIRE

Aiming his musket.

It's young Hawkins!

SMOLLETT

Get down, boy, get down.

DR. LIVESEY
Jim, Jim, climb over. Come on, lad!
Jim climbs over.
SQUIRE
Thank God you're safe!
SMOLLETT
How did you manage to keep away from them?
DR. LIVESEY
You are alright, aren't you?
JIM
I'm fine, really, I'm fine!
DR. LIVESEY
We saw you escape. What happened?
They all gather around Jim.
JIM
There's a man living on this island. His name is Ben Gunn.
SQUIRE
Some poor soul lives on this island, you say?
JIM
Yes, Ben Gunn, and he seems to have something to tell you!
SMOLLETT
Back to your posts!
*While everybody makes ready for the
attack, Jim talks to Dr. Livesey.*
REDRUTH
Here they come, sir!
There is a wild cry from off stage as the pirates charge.
SMOLLETT
Back to your firing positions, men! Jim, take cover!
Dr. Livesey shoots.
JIM
I'll stay and fight, sir.

SMOLLETT
Good lad!
Shouting above the noise, Squire runs out
of stockade. Smollett stops him.
SQUIRE
Come out and fight, cowards!
SMOLLET
No, get back. It might be a trick.
Jim lights the lantern.
Don't light the lantern!
DR. LIVESEY
No, Jim!!!
A shot rings out from the catwalk and knocks the
lantern into the barrel, which catches fire. Smoke
fills the stockade. Smollet fires a shot up into the
catwalk and the body of a pirate falls onto the stage.
The rest of the pirates now storm into view.
SMOLLETT
Out, lads, and fight them in the open!
The pirates lock swords with Dr. Livesey, Anderson,
Squire and Redruth. Two more pirates enter as the fighting
continues. Jim is attacked by Merry; he picks up a sword to
defend himself. In the midst of all this, Anderson douses the
fire with a bucket of water. A canon ball bursts overhead.
Retreat!
As the rest retreat to the stockade, Jim runs and
attacks three pirates and chases them off. As pirates
retreat, gun shots are fired from the stockade.
SQUIRE
After them, lads, don't let them get away!
A pirate returns and is about to kill the squire. Redruth
steps in and takes the blow; the pirate is chased
off. They carry Redruth back into the stockade.
REDRUTH
Be I going, Doctor?

DR. LIVESEY
You are going home Tom.
REDRUTH
I wish I had another lick at them with the gun first.
SQUIRE
Kneeling.
Tom, I was a bloody fool to bring you here.
Say you forgive me, won't you?
REDRUTH
Would that be respectful like, from me to you,
Squire? Howsoever, so be it, amen!
Pause
It would be nice if someone read a prayer. It's the custom, Sir.
SQUIRE
Yes, yes, of course...
DR. LIVESEY
Looking up.
He's gone.
Chantey Man sings.
IN THE BLUSTERY WIND
Jim breaks away.
SMOLLETT
Don't you take on, lad.
JIM
I wish I had never seen that map. This Is all my fault.
SMOLLETT
All's well with him; no fear for a hand that's been cut down
doing his duty. It mayn't be good divinity, but it's a fact.
*They cover Redruth. A cannon shell lands
near enough to Smollett to wound him.*
LIVESEY
Rushes to him
Smollett's been hit!

SMOLLETT
Come high tide we will be in range of the cannon.
Someone must cut the Hispaniola adrift.
SQUIRE
Take cover, here comes another one!
Explosion. Everybody ducks. In the chaos, Jim
surreptitiously leaves the stockade. Redruth
rises and becomes Chanteyman.
DR. LIVESEY
Everyone alright?
SQUIRE
Where's Jim?
CHANTEYMAN
Sings
HORAW HOO
Lights come up on Jim.
JIM
To the audience.
There was no return of the mutineers. I ran to where
I knew Ben Gunn kept his little boat. It was extremely
small, even for me. I had never before seen a coracle,
and I suspect Ben Gunn's was the worst ever made by
man. I waited for darkness, then shouldered the coracle
and groped my way out of the hollow and made my way
to the shore. I pushed out into the waves and made my
way to the Hispaniola. The schooner had swung round
to the ebb — her bow and the mooring rope were now
before me. The only lights on board were in the cabin.

THE HISPANIOLA DECK

Israel Hands staggers up on deck. He is very drunk.
O'Brien equally drunk, follows him on. He is singing.
"THEY CALL HIM HANGING JOHNNY."

HANDS

The Devil! You've cast us adrift!

O'BRIEN

I never did, you pillock!

HANDS

You're a damned liar! You've set us adrift! You'll
answer to Silver for this little prank!

O'BRIEN

Watch your mouth! Don't call me a
liar! I never done it, I tell ye!

HANDS

Lifting the cut hawser.

What's this then? Scotch mist? You cut
the blessed mooring rope !

O'BRIEN

Say I did it one more time, and I'll slit
your gizzard, so help me I will.

HANDS

You cut the hawser, you nincompoop!

O'BRIEN

That's it! That's it!

He draws a cutlass and dives at Hands.

HANDS

Fool! Silver will have you roasted on a spit!

*Hands draws his cutlass and the two men fight. During
the fight, O'Brien finds a bottle and breaks it over
Hands' head. Hands kicks O'Brien in the face. Anyway,
it is a dirty fight, ending with O'Brien being fatally
stabbed. Hands staggers away from O'Brien's body
and hits his head on some rigging, knocking himself
out. After a moment, Jim climbs over the side of the
ship. He does not immediately see the two men.*

JIM
(Cautiously)
Anyone aboard? Hello, anyone aboard?
Hands groans.
Israel Hands!
HANDS
Was it yourself who cut us adrift?
JIM
It was.
HANDS
Give me that brandy, boy.
Jim gives the bottle to Hands.
JIM
Here.
HANDS
Thanks, mate.
JIM
Are you badly hurt?
HANDS
Taking a swig.
I'll live.If that doctor was aboard, I'd be right enough in
a couple of turns, but I don't have no manner of luck,
you see. Where mought you have come from?
JIM
I've come aboard to take possession of this
ship, Mr. Hands, and you'll please regard me
as your captain until further notice.
Hands starts to laugh.
By the by, I can't have these colors, Mr. Hands, so by
your leave, I'll strike 'em. Better none than these.
Jim goes to the color line and takes down the "Jolly Roger."
There's an end to Captain Silver! God save the King!
HANDS
S'pose we talks?

JIM
Say on, Mr. Hands.
Looking at O'Brien.
Now, look here, you gives me food and drink and a
old scarf or 'ankecher to tie my wound up, you do,
and I'll tell you how to sail this 'ere boat back to the
mooring, and that's about square all round, I take it.
JIM
We are not returning to the old mooring. I'm going to
make for the North Inlet and beach her quietly there.
HANDS
To be sure you are. Why, I ain't sich a infernal lubber
after all. I can see, can't I? I've tried my fling, I have,
and I've lost, and it's you has the wind of me. North
Inlet? Why, I haven't no choice, not I! I'd help you sail
her up to Execution Dock, by thunder! So I would.
JIM
Taking out his pistol.
Very well, Mr. Hands, but one false move
and I'll blow you to kingdom come!
HANDS
Aye, aye, Cap'n. Easy, easy... Stand by to 'oist the jib.
Points to the rope.
It's that there rope over there. I reckons you can 'andle that.
*Jim goes to the indicated rope and starts to
pull. While his back is turned, Hands crawls to
O'Brien's body and retrieves his knife.*
Now, head her away from the wind till the sails fills.
Jim goes to the wheel. The sail fills with wind.
There you go, lad, now she's up and running.
You be quite the regular sea-dog!
Jim ties the wheel in place and returns to Hands.
There's one little thing that's a worry to me — my
old shipmate, O'Brien. S'pose you was to heave him
overboard. I don't reckon him ornamental now, do you?

JIM

I'm not strong enough and I don't like the
job; and there he lies, for me.

HANDS

This here's an unlucky ship. There's a power of men
been killed. I never seen sich dirty luck, not I.

(In a weak voice)

Cap'n, keep a weather eye open for reefs.

*He sighs and seems to pass out. Jim crosses to the side of
the ship and looks off. Hands rises slowly, pulls out his knife
and dives at Jim, who ducks out of the way, but not before
Hands cuts him. After avoiding Hands, Jim manages to climb
the mast. Hands climbs after him. Jim grabs a rope on a
pulley and slides down across the stage. Jim points his pistol.*

JIM

One more step, Mr. Hands, and I'll blow your
brains out! Dead men don't bite, you know.

HANDS

Jim, Jim, I reckon we're fouled, you and me, and we'll
have to sign articles. So as I don't have no luck, I
reckon I'll have to strike, which comes hard, you see,
for a master mariner to a ship's younker like you.

*In a flash Hands goes to throw the knife, Jim
screams and fires, killing Hands. Hands falls, The
ship runs aground. Jim slides to the deck.*

JIM

To the audience.

With the Hispaniola finally beached in the North inlet.
I let myself drop softly overboard; the water scarcely
reached my waist. I waded ashore. Then I set my face
for the long trek homeward to the block house and my
companions. The stockade, all I could think of now was
how to get back to the stockade, my friends and safety.

As the lights come up, it is almost dawn.

THE STOCKADE

JIM

Squire Trelawney... Dr. Livesey!

The parrot squawks, "Pieces of eight! Pieces of eight!" The pirates enter and surround Jim with the platforms. Jim makes a dash for the outer wall. and is stopped by Merry, who hurls him to the floor.

SILVER

Entering

Who goes? So, here's Jim Hawkins, shiver my timbers! Dropped in, like, eh? Well I take that friendly.

JIM

Where are Captain Smollett and Squire Trelawney? What have you done with them?

MERRY

Moving to kill Jim.

Silence, you little bilge rat! We should have done this long time ago.

SILVER

Easy, mate, easy! Before you slits his throat, let's give the lad a choice as to what side he wants to be on — according to pirate law. To answer your question, Mr. Hawkins, this morning, realizing that they 'ad no chance here, down came Doctor Livesey with a flag of truce. "Cap'n Silver, you're sold out and the ship's gone" says he. We looked out, and by thunder, the ship was gone! "Let's bargain," says the doctor. So we bargained, and here we are: stores, brandy, stockade and everything. And we agreed to let them go their own way on this here island. Now, if you think you are included in that there treaty, here's the last word that was said: "How many are you," I says, "to leave?" "Four," says he "and one wounded. As for that boy, I don't know where he is, confound him," says he. "Nor, I don't much care. We're about sick of him." So, Mr. Hawkins, I suggest that you sign articles and come along side of us.

JIM

Is that all?

SILVER

Well, it's all that you're to hear, my son.

JIM

And now I am to choose?

SILVER

And now you are to choose, and you may lay to that.

JIM

Let the worst come. It's little I care. But there's a thing
or two I have to tell you. You are in a bad way — ship
lost, treasure lost, men lost, your whole business gone to
wreck; and if you want to know who did it — it was I!

DIRK

Why, you little rat!

MERRY

Let's string him up!

MORGAN

Aye, by the heels.

SILVER

To Dirk and Merry.

Hold your words!

JIM

I was in the apple barrel — I heard everything you said the
night we sighted land, and told every word. It was I who
cut the hawser and killed the men you had aboard her.

SILVER

Hands and O'Brien dead?

JIM

I killed them and I brought that ship where you'll never see
her more. The laugh's on my side. Kill me or spare me.
But one thing I'll say, if you spare me, I'll let bygones be
bygones, and when you fellows are in court for piracy, I'll
save you all I can. Kill me and do yourselves no good, or
spare me and keep a witness to save you from the gallows.

MORGAN
Advancing with cutlass.
Let's do for him, I say!
PIRATES
Moving forward to grab Jim.
Aye!
*Morgan raises his cutlass to strike at Jim. Silver roughly
disarms Morgan, takes the cutlass and menaces the pirates.*
SILVER
Avast, Tom Morgan.
The pirates stop in their tracks. To Morgan.
Take a cutlass, him that dares, and I'll
see the color of his inside.
*Still, no one moves. The pirates go
back to their original positions.*
I like that boy, now; I never seen a better boy than that.
He's turned out to be more a man than any of you.
And what I say is this: let me see him that'll lay a hand
on him — that's what I say, and you may lay to it.
The pirates retreat to a corner. Silver Pulls Jim aside.
SILVER
Now look here, you're within half a plank of
death, and what's a long sight worse, of torture.
You're my last card says I and I'm yours.
JIM
You mean all's lost
SILVER
Ship's gone, neck gone — that's the size of it. I'll
save your life — if I can. But, see here, Jim — tit
for tat — you save Long John from swinging.
JIM
What I can do, that I'll do.

SILVER

Bandaging Jim's shoulder.

It's a bargain! You speak up plucky. Understand me,
Jim, I'm on the squire's side now. I know when the
game is up, I do; and I know a lad that's staunch.

LIVESEY

Offstage.

Blockhouse, ahoy!

Dr Liveseye enters.

SILVER

The doctor, you know, gave me the treasure map, Jim.
Top of the morning to you, Sir! Bright and early, to be sure;
and it's the early bird, as the saying goes, that gets the
rations. Men, shake up your timbers and help Dr. Livesey.

Turning to Jim

Part of the bargain, Jim. All a-doing well, your patients
was — all well and merry. We've quite a surprise
for you, too, sir. We've a little stranger here.

LIVESEY

Not Jim?

SILVER

The very same Jim as ever was.

LIVESEY

Well, well...duty first. Let us overhaul these patients of yours.
Well, George, how goes it?. Did you take that
medicine? Did he take that medicine, men?

PIRATES

Aye, he took it sure... Aye, aye, sir... He did for
sure... I saw him take it!... That he did!

LIVESEY

Because, you see, I'm a doctor and I make it a point
of honor not to lose a man for the gallows.

LIVESEY

Handing them some medicine

Well, that's done for today. Now I wish to talk to the boy.

PIRATES

No... etc.

SILVER

Silence! You be crossing me again. Hawkins,
will you give me your word of honor as a young
gentleman...not to slip your cable?

Jim nods

Then, doctor, you just step outside and once you're there,
I'll let the boy go to yarn with you. Good day to you, Sir.

Livesey exits the stockade.

PIRATES

Are you mad!... What are you thinking of?... You ain't letting
that bilge rat out!... He'll run off... They'll break the treaty,

SILVER (CONT'D)

No, by thunder! Who's cap'n here?

(Winks at Jim)

Takes the noose off Jim's neck and glares at Merry.

Now get things shipshape.

*Merry hands Morgan a musket and indicates to
Morgan to stay behind and keep watch. Silver
crosses out of the blockhouse to Dr. Livesey.*

SILVER

You'll make a note of this here also, Doctor, and the
boy'll tell you how I saved his life. You'll please bear
in mind it's not my life only now...it's that boy's into
the bargain; and you'll speak me fair, Doctor, and give
me a bit o' hope to go on, for the sake of mercy.

LIVESEY

(Sarcastically)

Why, John, you're not afraid?

SILVER

Doctor, I'm no coward, but I'll own up fairly,
I've the shakes upon me for the gallows. I'll
step aside and leave you and Jim alone.

He moves away a little.

76

LIVESEY

So, Jim, here you are. I cannot find it in my heart to
blame you, but this much I will say, when Captain
Smollet was well, you'd dared not have gone off; and
when he was hit, it was downright cowardly to run.

JIM

(Softly)

But, Doctor, I got the ship, part by luck and part by risking,
and she lies in the North Inlet, on the southern beach.

LIVESEY

(Taken aback)

Every step, it's you that saves our lives. You found
out the plot; you found Ben Gunn — the best deed
you ever did. Jim, we'll make a run for it.

JIM

No, doctor, I passed my word.

(Pause)

I can die-and I dare say I deserve it-but what I fear is torture.

LIVESEY

Come Jim, run, just run and we're out of here.

JIM

No, you know right well you wouldn't do the thing
yourself...neither you nor the squire nor the captain,
and no more will I. Silver trusts me. I should have
been dead by now if Silver hadn't stood by me
and besides I passed my word, so back I go.

LIVESEY

To Silver

Silver... Silver! I'll give you a piece of advice.
Don't you be in a hurry after that treasure.

Silver crosses back.

SILVER

(Realizing something's up)

Sir, as between man and man, that's too late.

LIVESEY

If we both get alive out of this wolf trap, I'll do
my best to save you, short of perjury.

SILVER

You couldn't say more, I'm sure, Sir,
not if you was my own mother.

LIVESEY

Keep that boy close beside you. I'm off to
seek help for you. Good bye, Jim.

Livesey exits.

The pirates enter with the Black Spot.

SILVER

To Dirk

Step up, lad. I won't eat you. I know the
rules, I do; I won't hurt a deputation.

*They push Dirk towards Silver. Dirk hands Silver
a tiny piece of paper. Silver looks at it.*

The black spot! I thought so.Deposed!.Very pretty
wrote. So you'd be bucking for Cap'n, George Merry?
Why look here, now; this ain't lucky! You've gone and
cut this out of a Bible. What fool's cut a Bible?

Pirates react like scared children.

MORGAN

It were Dirk.

MERRY

Quit that tack, John.

SILVER

Ignoring him

Dirk, was it? Then Dirk can get to prayers.
He's seen his slice of luck, has Dirk.

MERRY

Belay that talk, John Silver.

SILVER

I thought you said you knowed the rules. I'm still cap'n till you outs me with your grievances and I reply; in the meantime, your black spot ain't worth a biscuit. After that, we'll see.

MERRY

First, you made a hash of this cruise. You'll be bold to say no to that. Second, you let the enemy out o' this here trap for nothing. Third, you wouldn't let us go at them upon the march. Oh, we see through you, John Silver; you want to play both sides, that's what's wrong with you. And then, there's this here boy.

SILVER

Is that all?

SILVER

You say this cruise is bungled. We're that near the gibbet that my neck's stiff with thinking of it. Thanks to you, Merry, and the others. As for this boy, isn't he a 'ostage? Are we going to waste a 'ostage? No, not us, he might be our last chance. Besides, he's the only one who knows where the ship is. Kill this boy? Not me, mates! And as for why I made the bargain — look you there.

He throws the chart on the ground.

That's why!

The men fall on the chart, except for Merry, and pass it from hand to hand.

DIRK

Flint's Fist!

MORGAN

That's Flint's, sure enough. J.F. and a score below with a clove hitch to it; so he done ever.

MERRY

Mighty pretty. But how are we to get away with it, and us with no ship?

SILVER

How? Why, how do I know? You had ought to tell me that, you and the rest of the crew, that lost me the schooner with your interference, burn you! But not you, you can't, you hain't got the invention of a cockroach. You lost the ship; I found the treasure. Who's the better man? I resign, by thunder! Elect whom you please to be your cap'n now. I'm done with it.

MORGAN

We want you, Silver.

PIRATES

Aye, aye, Silver.

SILVER

So that's the toon, is it? George, I reckon you'll have to wait another turn, my son. Lucky for you that I'm not a revengeful man. Now let's go find this 'ere treasure.

CHANTEYMAN

Sings

A NICE BIT OF GOLD.

Silver and the company exit to begin the treasure hunt.

SILVER

Now then let's have a squint at this here chart.

MORGAN

Read it to us, Long John.

SILVER

Spy-glass shoulder, bearing a point to the North of Northeast.

Pointing

Mizzenmast Hill. East by Southeast. Tall tree. Cave.

MORGAN

Looking at the chart

A tall tree is the principal mark.

MERRY

Aye, but where's the cave? There are plenty
of tall trees, but where's the cave?

JIM

Pointing

That tree is taller than the rest.

SILVER

Young Hawkins is right.

BEN GUNN

Singing, off stage

FIFTEEN MEN ON A DEAD MAN'S CHEST...

MERRY

It's Flint's ghost!

SILVER

Avast there, George Merry, Flint's dead, and
the dead don't come back, I think!

MERRY

But, that was Flint's voice!

MORGAN

Aye, and his song!

DIRK

I heard it, too!

MORGAN

It was Flint's way of singing.

MERRY

And 'is tones, too!

SILVER

Cowards! There's seven hundred thousand pounds not
more than a few feet from here. When ever did a gentleman
o' fortune show his stern to that much money for a boozy
old seaman with a blue mug on him, and him dead, too?

MERRY

Belay there, John!

DIRK

Don't you cross a sperrit!

SILVER

I told you, I told you, you spoiled your Bible, Dirk.
Come on, mates. There was an echo. Now, no

man ever seen a sperrit with a shadow. Well
then, what's he doing with an echo to him?
MERRY
(Much relieved)
That's so. You've a head upon your shoulders,
John, and no mistake. Come to think of it, it was like
Flint's voice, but not just so clear-away like it.
MORGAN
Aye, it was like...like...
SILVER
Thar's the cave, lads! Come on, mates,
the treasure must be here abouts!

THE CAVE

DIRK
(Nervously)
It's dark in there.
MORGAN
Look, there's an old lamp.
Dirk takes it.
SILVER
Bring it here, lad.
*Silver gives the tinder box to Jake who lights
the lamp. They enter the cave..*
In, Dirk, in!
DIRK
Don't push me, Merry. I'm going as fast as I can.
MERRY
Get a move on!
DIRK
The ground is slippery.
MORGAN
I've a creepy feeling we are being watched.

SILVER

Don't talk foolish.

A gust of wind blows the torch out. Silver strikes the tinder box.The following is played in the dark.

MORGAN

That's an omen. This is your fault, Dirk, for cutting a Bible.

DIRK

Quit saying that. Who's got the tinder box?

SILVER

I gave it to Merry.

MERRY

No, you didn't.

SILVER

You can't be trusted with anything, George Merry.

MORGAN

It's so dark, it's like looking at a black cat in a coal cellar.

DIRK

Quit touching me, Merry,

MERRY

I'm not touching you.

DIRK

Don't lie.

MORGAN

He's not. He's over here with me.

So who's got the tinder box. Oh! I have.

DIRK

What's that on my neck?

*Morgan strikes the tinder box.*SILVER

Keep quite still, lad... Spiders!

DIRK

Whaaaaaaaa! Get them off me. I can't abide spiders.

MORGAN
The cave's full of spiders.
Morgan is frantically trying to light the torch. Dirk is leaping
about, brushing spiders off. The torch is lit. (Pause) Lights up.
SILVER
When you dainty milk-maids have stopped
dancing, perhaps we can get on.
Dirk steps on a device and triggers a skeleton.
It rises from the floor behind Dirk, and
points to the location of the treasure.
DIRK
Whaaaaaaa!
SILVER
By the powers, a skeleton!
MERRY
He was a seaman, least ways, this is good sea-cloth.
SILVER
Aye, aye, like enough; you wouldn't look to find a bishop
here, I reckon. But what sort of way is that for bones to lie.
MORGAN
It ain't natur'l!
SILVER
I've taken a notion into my old numskull, this is one
of old Flint's jokes. Six came ashore when he buried
the treasure — none came back. Could this be one of
the six? Let's see. Long bones...and yellow hair?
MERRY
Allerdyes! Aye, that would be Allerdyes. He owed me
money, he did, and took my knife ashore with him, he did.
MORGAN
It should be lying around. Flint warn't the man to pick a
seaman's pocket, and rodents, I guess, would leave it be.
SILVER
Aye, that's true.

DIRK

Feeling around the bones.

There ain't a thing left here, not a copper doit
nor a baccy box. It don't look nat'ral to me.

SILVER

We should search here.

*The men move in and pull out a treasure
chest from a trap in the floor.*

It's here!

DIRK

We've found it!

MORGAN

Flint's treasure!

MERRY

It's locked.

SILVER

George Merry, when brains were handed out you
must have been behind the door. Open it.

MERRY

With what?

SILVER

Use your musket.

MERRY

Stand back, mates.

*He fires his gun at the lock. They open
the chest. Holding up a rock*

Rocks!!!!

SILVER

What?

MORGAN

Rocks!

MERRY

We've been tricked, mates. You done this, John Silver,
you and this boy. You knew it all along, didn't you?
Look in the face of him, you'll see it wrote there!

SILVER
Pulling a pistol.
Ah, Merry, standing for cap'n again?
You're a pushing lad, to be sure.
MERRY
Mates, there's two of them; one's the old cripple that
brought us here and blundered us down to this, the
other's this cub that I mean to have the heart of.
JIM
Long John?
*Merry pulls a knife to cut Jim's throat. Silver
shoots and kills Merry. Jim breaks free.*
DIRK
Shouts
Silver!
*He shoots Silver. Silver falls. Suddenly there is gunfire all
around. Dr. Livesey, Captain Smollet and Squire Trelawney
drive off the pirates. Jim runs to the body of Silver.*
LIVESEY
Are you alright, Jim?
JIM
They've killed Long John.
SMOLLETT
Silver dead? Well, I can't say I'm sorry. The man
was a blackguard, even if he was a good cook.
JIM
(In tears)
He saved my life.
LIVESEY
None of us live forever, Jim.
SQUIRE
(Trying to cheer up Jim)
Livesey, allow me to say a few words. Jim, the man
was a prodigious villain and impostor, a monstrous
impostor. However, he is now before his god, where

all his sins will be washed away. I must add that although the rest of you could only see the bad side of him, I knew in my heart of hearts that there was a good man lurking underneath that coarse exterior.

During this, unnoticed by the squire, Silver sits up.

Had he survived today I would have been proud to have him as my friend. Not only that, Jim, I could have found a worthwhile place for him in my estate. A place of trust, a place where he could have been proud. Yes, you may be amazed but it is true I would have done my best for him...

SILVER

Thank you kindly, Squire. It's nice to be so well thought of.

SQUIRE

Well I...I...I!!!

JIM

I thought you were hit!

SILVER

I was, right in little Davy Jones here.

He holds up the flask. Everyone laughs. Ben Gunn, draped in jewelry from head to foot, slides down a vine from above or he enters on a goat cart. Should be a great entrance.

By the powers, Ben Gunn, so it was you that was singing. I thought I recognized that voice.
Well, you're a nice one to be sure.

BEN

How do, Mr. Silver? Pretty well, thank ye, says I...

SILVER

(Laughs)

To think it was you as done me!

BEN GUNN

Where's Flint's treasure, says you? In Ben Gunn's cave says I. Three years it took me to take it there. Three years, day by day. Every little bit of Flint's treasure, it's all there. Every last coin. It'll buy my passage back to England, says I.

SILVER

You can lay to that, and no mistake.

BEN

Oh, yes, Mr. Silver, I said to Squire Trelawney.
"Let's bargain — fair shares of Flint's treasure and
a free passage home," says I. "Done," says he.

JIM

And he'll keep his word.

SQUIRE

Jim, my boy, now that we have the Hispaniola, all we have
to do is load her up and set sail home for England.

Silver grabs Anderson's pistol.

BEN

Exiting; screaming.

Ahh! He's got a gun.

SILVER

Well, Jim, I reckon this is where we must part company.

JIM

Why, Long John?

SILVER

I can't go back to England to get my neck stretched and
be sun dried at Execution Dock. No, I'd rather die here.

Silver puts the pistol to his head.

DR. LIVESEY

Silver, put that gun away. There's no need for
that. You saved young Jim's life. For that we
are grateful and we won't prosecute you.

SILVER

You mean I'm to be a free man, sir? Give
us a hand up there, Squire.

SQUIRE

Helping Silver up.

Silver, against my better judgment, I'll do as Livesey said.
But let me tell you, sir, dead men hang about your neck

like mill-stones. One more transgression from you and I personally will prosecute to the fullest letter of the law.

SILVER

Thank you kindly, sir.

SQUIRE

How dare you thank me! It is a gross dereliction of my duty. Stand back. Come, let's get back to the ship..

The lights fade to a pin-spot on Jim.

The chanteyman sets up the Hispaniola as Jim speaks.

So that should have been the end of my story. However, there was one final event which will live with me for the rest of my life. Having loaded all the treasure on board we set sail for a port in Spanish America to take on a new crew and supplies for the journey home to England. Two days into the passage we sheltered in a beautiful land-locked bay.

A penny whistle plays mood music.

The night was hot and sultry, and not being able to get back to sleep, I went up on deck.

Lights come up on the stern area of the Hispaniola.

DECK OF HISPANIOLA

Jim looks over the side as the tarpaulin on the longboat moves back, revealing Silver with all his possessions ready to set sail.

JIM

Long John, what are you doing?

SILVER

Ah! I was a thinking of taking a nap in this here boat, the night being so hot and all...

JIM

Then why don't you sleep on the deck?

SILVER

Ah...I needs the solitude...

JIM

Why are all your belongings in the boat?

SILVER

Jim, my son, you and me is mates, ain't we? I can't go back to England and stand trial...

JIM

But Dr. Livesey said you'd not be prosecuted...

SILVER

I know'd what he said and I trust him with my life, but...

JIM

Do you expect to get away with this, Long John?

SILVER

Well, that depends on whether you was to cry out and alert the others.

JIM

Why shouldn't I?

SILVER

It's the squire, he talks three ways to Sunday; he don't know when to shut up!

JIM

He'll keep his word. I promise you. I will go and get him now and make him say that to your face.

SILVER

You're right, young Jim, you do that and old Long John will bless you forever.

Silver hides "Little Davy Jones" in his belongings.
Now before you go and get the Squire, would you do an old sea dog a favor and get me my brandy flask out of that sack there?

JIM

Turning around.
This one?
Jim looks in the sack for the flask.

SILVER

Aye, lad! You and me 'as been as close as two peas in a pod, but we have to part.

*Long John, as he speaks, slowly draws the dagger out
of his boot and suddenly pulls Jim backwards placing
the dagger on Jim's throat. He slowly lets Jim go.*

JIM

Without turning

I knew you couldn't do it.

SILVER

Aye lad, I couldn't... Jim, if I'm to change my ways
I must do it on my own, start a new life for myself.
Who knows, maybe I will become a parson.

JIM

(Ruefully)

So this is farewell?

SILVER

No, no... Well, yes, you could put it like that... Shiver my
timbers, why didn't I think of this before? You come with
me! We could have a grand life together. What do you
want to go back to England for? It always rains there. We
could make for Portobello in the South Americas, where
the sun is always shining. We could live like fighting cocks
there. We'd buy a plantation with servants to look after us.
We'd do what we want. Free as a feather in the wind. We
could sail the seven seas, the whole world would be our
oyster. Come with me, lad. All we need is a couple of bags
of gold to set us right. What with me and my experience
and you and your ten toes, what a fine team we'd make.

JIM

Silver, as far as my experience goes, you have
taught me the value of true friends. But as for
my ten toes, I propose to keep them.

*Jim unties the boat and pushes Silver away from the
ship. From the back of the boat in the moonlight, streams
a blue silk which will represent the wake of the boat.*

SILVER

(Stung)

So be it. Good luck to you, matey. Remember
me when you are a lord in parliament.

*When Silver is a little way off he throws an
object to Jim. It is the brandy flask.*

Look after Little Davy Jones for me.

Silver laughs.

Thankey lad..... Oh Jim— tell the squire I've
borrowed one of his bags of gold!

JIM

Holding up the bag of gold

You mean this one !

Silver reacts and then knowingly laughs.

Ben Gunn appears with cannon.

BEN GUNN

Caught you, Mr. Silver. You are not going to
get away with this! Say goodbye, Mr. Silver.
I'm going to blow you out of the water!

Raises the match.

SILVER

Let's be reasonable Ben.....etc

*The cannon fires and we hear the cannonball fly
through the air. We see the cannonball land behind
Silver, a jet of dry ice and smoke create the splash
and the other half of the audience gets wet.*

SILVER

Missed !

THE END

INDEX

in order of appearance in the script

Stay a bit.	Wait a moment!
Men before the mast	Crew.
Stern	Back of ship.
The "deuce."	The devil.
Bow	Front of the ship.
Spring line.	
Stern Line.	Ropes are tied diagonally from the bow and the stern to a point on the dock and made fast to keep the ship from moving forward or backwards.
Capstan	A device on the deck that can be used to haul up the anchor chain.
Helm	Ship's wheel.
Splice	Knotting a rope on itself to stop it from fraying {back splice} or to create a loop,{eye splice}.
Land lubber	Not a seaman. Land lover.
Blue fire	The worst fire ever.
Dab Hand	Expert.
Dang	Damn.
Stow	Put away.
Foc's'le hands	Another term for crew.
Watch your bilge	A threat, to the body.
Flower of the flock	The best.
Berth	Sleeping space.
Double Dutchman	18th century insult.
Focs'le	Crew's living quarters.
Athwart	From side to side.
Larboard	To the left.
Starboard	To the right.

Flag of truce	White flag requiring a cease fire.
Trader	A ship that carries cargo to be traded.
Marooned	Abandoned
Hitch	Knot
Shiver my Timbers	Oath: To break into pieces'.
Coracle	Small round boat.
Lee shore	A shore lying on the leeward side of a ship (and on to which a ship could be blown in foul weather).The wind would be blowing towards the shore.

PLEASE!PLEASE!

PUT THE PLAY BACK IN PLAY.

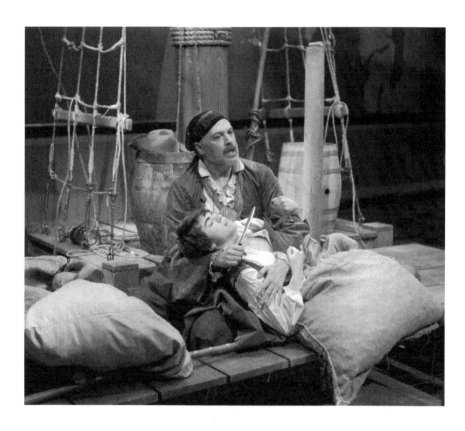

Tom Hewitt, as Long John Silver, and Noah E. Galvin as Jim Hawkins in "Treasure Island." Photos by Ken Howard.

L-R Josh Clayton, Rod Brogan, Liberty Smiling, Steven Blanchard, Rocco Sisto, Michael Gabriel Goodfriend, Kenneth Tigar.Philip Willingham, Tom Hewitt, John Ahlin, Noah Galvin, Ken Schatz. L-R, Josh Clayton, Rod Brogan, Kenneth Tigar, Liberty Smiling, Michael Gabriel Goodfriend.

L-R Josh Clayton, Rod Brogan, Kenneth Tigar, Liberty Sterling.

Michael Gabriel Goodfriend

Made in the USA
Middletown, DE
22 June 2023